Tony was doing some fast arithmetic in his head as he showered. That night, after dinner, he would take another "magic vitamin." That would leave him with only four. It was clear to Tony that he shouldn't stop taking them now, not when they were doing him so much good.

I'd better stop off at the gym tonight or tomorrow night to see Lou, he told himself. *I don't want to run out of these pills now, not when we've got a meet this Saturday. Everyone will be out there, expecting great things from me, especially Dad.*

If I'd waited and taken Dr. Griffin's advice, I'd probably still be sitting on the bench, Tony reminded himself.

It wasn't until he got back to his locker and started to get dressed that a little voice in the back of his head reminded him that he didn't really know what was in those pills.

I shouldn't just go and buy more of them, he thought uneasily as he slipped his polo shirt over his head. *Not without asking more about them. Not without finding out what these magic vitamins really are.*

Bantam Books in the Sweet Valley High series
Ask your bookseller for the books you have missed

FRANCINE PASCAL'S

SWEET VALLEY High ®

CHEATING TO WIN

Written by
Kate William

Created by
FRANCINE PASCAL

BANTAM BOOKS
NEW YORK · TORONTO · LONDON · SYDNEY · AUCKLAND

RL 6, age 12 and up

CHEATING TO WIN
A Bantam Book / July 1991

Sweet Valley High is a registered trademark of Francine Pascal

Conceived by Francine Pascal

*Produced by Daniel Weiss Associates, Inc.
33 West 17th Street
New York, NY 10011*

Cover art by James Mathewuse

ISBN 0-553-29145-9

Published simultaneously in the United States and Canada

Bantam Books are published by Bantam Books, a division
of Bantam Doubleday Dell Publishing Group, Inc. Its trademark, consisting of the words "Bantam Books" and the por-
trayal of a rooster, is Registered in U.S. Patent and
Trademark Office and in other countries. Marca Registrada.
Bantam Books, 666 Fifth Avenue, New York, New York
10103.

PRINTED IN THE UNITED STATES OF AMERICA

OPM   0 9 8 7 6 5 4 3 2 1

CHEATING TO WIN

One

Todd Wilkins looked at Elizabeth Wakefield with a twinkle in his coffee-colored eyes. "Don't tell me I get to eat lunch alone with my girlfriend!" he teased as they set their trays down at a table in the crowded lunchroom. It was noon on Wednesday, and most of Sweet Valley High's student body was jammed into the cafeteria.

Elizabeth laughed. "You may be right. We *are* alone, for the first time in ages," she said.

"Well, we promised we'd do it. Our friends will probably be mad at us," Todd said as he put his hand over hers. "But I get half an hour alone with you. And that makes it worth it."

Elizabeth blushed. Even though she and Todd had been seeing each other steadily for a long time, she still found their relationship very

1

romantic. She was as glad as Todd was that they'd managed to sneak past the crowded table where their closest friends were sitting, to steal some time alone. Both Elizabeth and Todd were popular and outgoing, devoted to their friends and extracurricular activities, so it wasn't always easy to get privacy at Sweet Valley High! Elizabeth had been bemoaning her situation to her twin sister, Jessica, the night before. Of course, Jessica hadn't sympathized. "You and Todd are too serious as it is," was all she had said, with a toss of her golden-blond hair.

It just goes to show how different "identicals" can be, Elizabeth mused as she looked tenderly at Todd. "Too serious" were not words that made sense to Elizabeth Wakefield. Once she committed herself to something, such as her position as a writer for *The Oracle*, Sweet Valley High's student newspaper, or to someone, such as Todd, she committed herself heart and soul. Let Jessica play the field and flit from guy to guy. Elizabeth chose *not* to live life in the fast lane!

"OK," Todd said. "Now that I've finally got you alone, tell me how your day's been so far."

"Things were crazy at the *Oracle* meeting Mr. Collins organized this morning," Elizabeth told Todd as they began to eat their lunches. "A couple of staff writers have resigned and we've barely got enough people to cover school events. In fact, John Pfeifer asked me if I could help him out with the sports department for a while."

"Really? Well, you're a natural, Liz. You've done some great sports interviews, especially that profile of Claire Middleton."

Claire Middleton, who had recently moved to Sweet Valley, had fought for a position on the all-male football team, the Gladiators, and Elizabeth had covered the sensational story. "Yeah, I think it'll be fun," Elizabeth agreed. "John mentioned he might need me to help cover some of the big track meets coming up." She grinned. "So you'd better help me brush up on my sports-coverage skills!" Todd's sport was basketball, but he was such an avid fan, she knew he would be able to give her pointers on track as well.

"Uh, oh," Todd said suddenly, under his breath. "Don't look now, but I think our romantic, just-the-two-of-us lunch is about to be interrupted." Roger Barrett-Patman was looking around for a place to sit, and his gaze had fallen on their table.

A moment later Roger was pulling up a chair. He glanced from Todd to Elizabeth. "Hi, guys. Mind if I join you?"

Todd hesitated, as if he were actually going to ask Roger to sit at another table. But before he could speak Roger sat down. "I'm absolutely starving," he exclaimed as he unwrapped an enormous submarine sandwich. "Coach Feath-erston has been working us really hard lately.

I think I could eat twice what I usually eat and still lose weight."

Roger Barrett-Patman had been a friend of Elizabeth's for a long time. He was a good, solid guy, someone whose values Elizabeth very much admired. *It couldn't have been easy for Roger to trade places the way he did*, Elizabeth thought as she looked at him. Roger had been raised by his mother, who had had very little money. For a while he had helped pay the rent by working as a janitor after school. Then his mother had become seriously ill, and a mysterious benefactor began to give money to the Barretts. But even with the expert medical help the money had made possible, Roger's mother died, leaving Roger completely alone in the world. At least, that's what he had thought at first. But after her death an incredible secret had been revealed about her early life. Mrs. Barrett had once been romantically involved with Henry Patman's brother. Roger was in fact the illegitimate nephew of one of the richest men in the state of California!

Elizabeth and her classmates had watched Roger go from rags to riches. He had moved into the Patmans' mansion, and had learned to deal with his arrogant new cousin, Bruce Patman, the flashy senior whose license plates 1BRUCE1 revealed the enormity of his ego. Elizabeth knew that for Roger, running had been a great help throughout that turbulent time. He had been a star member of the track team

4

before his sudden change in status, and had remained a star member, despite all the turmoil caused by adjusting to his new life.

"John Pfeifer told me you may help him cover some track meets," Roger said to Elizabeth. He laughed. "Make sure to mention that at least one runner you know is exhausted. And we're still more than seven weeks away from the All-County meet!"

"That's right," Elizabeth said excitedly. "You'll be able to give me the whole inside story. Grueling practices, team gossip, all the juicy stuff I need to liven up my stories." Elizabeth was teasing, but Roger seemed to take her seriously.

"Grueling isn't the word," he responded. "The way the coach has been driving us, you'd think everyone, not just Tony Esteban, was heading for the Olympics." Roger shook his head. "It's weird how competitive a practice can get. But I guess that's sports, huh?"

"I don't know," Elizabeth answered. "I'm not sure high school sports have to be so extreme."

"Sure they do. If you want to win!" Roger grinned. He sat back and took a swig of soda. "Sorry, guys! I didn't mean to barge in on your lunch and go on about something only I happen to find thrilling. I guess I'm just a little keyed up."

"No problem." Todd laughed. "We love hearing the inside scoop."

5

"When's your next meet?" Elizabeth asked.

"We're up against Big Mesa this Saturday," Roger said. "Then we've got a meet almost every Saturday until the All-County." He shook his head. "The guy who's really under pressure is Tony. I meant it when I said he's heading for the Olympics. A few talent scouts have been coming to our practices, and I know they're not here to watch me!"

"You're a pretty good runner yourself, Roger," Todd replied.

"Yeah, but not like Tony." Roger pushed his hair back. "The great thing about Tony is that he's the sort of guy who doesn't let the pressure or the fame get to him. He's the same guy he was three years ago when he was just 'a runner with potential.' The only thing that's changed is that he gave up the soccer team to devote all of his energy to running."

"Yeah," Todd said, "but there's bound to be extra pressure on him this season."

"Sure," Roger replied. "But I think Tony can handle it. It's not often you find someone who's so good at a sport *and* so levelheaded about it."

Elizabeth didn't know Tony very well, but she had always liked him. He seemed to be a self-possessed guy, someone who seemed sure of who he was and what he wanted. You would never guess from his nonchalant, matter-of-fact demeanor that he was going to be so famous! "Maybe I should do a profile of him for *The Oracle* before the Olympic committee gets ahold of him!" Elizabeth said to Roger.

"Sure, why not?" Roger said, adding, "Excuse me for a second. I've got to get another ice-cream bar. Can I get either of you anything?"

Elizabeth and Todd both declined. They waited until Roger was out of earshot to talk about their plans for that afternoon.

"I don't care where we go or what we do," Todd said dramatically, taking her hands in his. "I just want some time with you."

"Let's see . . . we could go for a bicycle ride," Elizabeth mused.

"Great. Maybe we could ride to the beach," Todd replied. "I haven't seen you in that gorgeous blue bathing suit in a long time!"

"The beach sounds great," Elizabeth said. "I wonder if Roger wants to join us? It sounds as if he needs a break."

"But what about being alone, just the two of us? I thought this beach excursion was something special," Todd objected.

"Later," Elizabeth promised, her eyes twinkling. "We'll steal away for a romantic walk along the shore. I promise." Elizabeth saw that Todd seemed a bit disappointed, but she was sure he didn't really mind her inviting Roger along for that afternoon.

Roger came back to the table, his ice-cream bar already half-eaten. He thanked Elizabeth for her invitation but turned it down. "I have to

7

get some things straightened out at home," he said. "I've got a houseguest coming down from L.A. tomorrow. In fact, he's going to be a long-term houseguest." Roger finished off his ice cream and continued his story.

"It isn't anyone either of you guys know. My mom had a close friend named Denise Ferguson, who moved up to L.A. just before my mom got sick. Denise has a son named Mitch. He's thirteen now, but I haven't seen him in a while." Roger chuckled. "He'll probably surprise me in more ways than one."

"And he's coming to visit you?" Elizabeth asked.

Roger nodded. "Denise is having a rough time with Mitch. Mitch's dad died five years ago and he's never really gotten over it. He goes to school with some really tough kids, and apparently he's gotten in with their crowd. Last week he got suspended for drinking."

"Oh no," Elizabeth said softly. "He's only thirteen?"

"Yeah, isn't that sad? Denise isn't home much these days because she's got two jobs, and she thinks Mitch needs to be around someone who can be a positive role model for him. So she asked me if she could send Mitch to Sweet Valley for the five-week period of his suspension. She thinks it'll be good for him to get out of the city and away from the rough kids he hangs around with, and I guess she's hoping I can be some sort of positive influence on him."

"If anyone can, Roger, you can," Elizabeth said earnestly. After all, she thought, Roger had grown up in a similarly hard situation. "I'm sure you'll be able to help Mitch a lot!"

"Well, listen, if you two have any extra time . . ."

"Sure, Roger," Elizabeth replied. She didn't even stop to think about the promise she and Todd had made to spend more time together and to make fewer commitments to other people. But Elizabeth couldn't say no to a request such as Roger's. It sounded as if Mitch Ferguson could use all the friends he could get. She was so intent on Roger's story that she barely noticed Todd's tense expression.

"I'll tell you what. We're going to have a barbecue on Friday night, a sort of Welcome Mitch thing. Can you guys come?" Roger asked.

"Sure, that sounds great," Elizabeth agreed.

Todd nudged her under the table. "Liz," he said. But Roger was racing ahead with plans for the barbecue.

"Good. Ask Jessica, too, Liz. I'm going to invite Tony Esteban and Annie Whitman. I'd like there to be a bunch of people around to make Mitch feel at home."

"Well, you can count on us." It made Elizabeth proud to think that she and Todd were the kind of couple their friends could count on to be there for them—not like those annoying self-absorbed couples who always wanted to be alone.

Roger stood and picked up his tray. "Wish me luck," he added. "I'm not sure I'm ready to be a role model for a thirteen-year-old. At least, not for one who's already in serious trouble."

"Roger, you'll be great," Elizabeth assured him. She turned back to Todd as Roger walked off. "You don't mind about Friday night, do you?" she asked him.

"Why should I?" Todd said glumly. "Just because you and I made a promise to go somewhere romantic on Friday, just the two of us?"

Elizabeth bit her lip. *There's always Saturday night,* she objected inwardly. It wasn't like Todd to be so insistent. True, they'd promised each other they'd try for more time alone, but Elizabeth had thought Todd was only teasing when he had asked her to make the pact. Now it looked as if he had been serious about it!

Jessica was in a rotten mood when Elizabeth got back from the beach that afternoon.

"Look what Prince Albert did," she complained. "He chewed my brand-new blouse! I'm ready to kill him!"

Elizabeth laughed and looked down affectionately at the Wakefields' boisterous yellow Lab. Even though he was pretty big, he was still a puppy in spirit. "Maybe he needs to go to obedience school," she suggested.

Jessica tossed the blouse on her bed and snatched up her hairbrush. "He needs to replace my blouse," she said angrily.

Elizabeth hid a giggle. "Come on, Jess. Forgive him. Look at those big, sad eyes," she wheedled.

Jessica glanced down at Prince Albert, whose imploring expression could have made the fiercest person melt. "All right, all right," she muttered. "But tomorrow I'm putting a padlock on my door so he can't ruin anything else!"

Elizabeth shooed Prince Albert downstairs and sat down on her sister's bed. She looked around at the chaos her twin claimed was "casual clutter." With its chocolate-brown walls and complete lack of order, Jessica's bedroom was an unofficial Wakefield disaster area.

To think we were born only four minutes apart, Elizabeth thought. Four minutes could have been four years in their case. True, the girls were mirror images of each other. Their soft, wavy blond hair, eyes the sparkling blue-green of the Pacific Ocean, and lovely size-six figures made it difficult for some people to tell the two apart. But their friends could tell by the difference in the twins' styles. Jessica always wore the latest fashions; Elizabeth's taste in clothes was more conservative. Elizabeth always wore a watch; Jessica thought worrying about the time was definitely "un-California."

It would be hard to find two people with more different temperaments, too. Jessica shunned all the things Elizabeth valued, such as hard work, studying, and a few close, loyal friendships, in favor of cheerleading, dancing, and big groups of adoring guys. Though underneath it all the twins were extremely close and would do anything for each other. Jessica loved to tease her sister. Why write for the school paper when she could be a high-profile cheerleader? Why go steady when she could have dates with three different guys in one weekend?

"What's bugging you?" Elizabeth asked her sister. "Prince Albert can't be the only thing."

Jessica made a face. "Oh, it's this dumb Miss Teen Sweet Valley thing. I actually have to *work* at it! I didn't think I'd have to go places and talk to people and make speeches and do all sorts of boring stuff. At least if things had worked out with Frazer I'd have gotten something good out of it all."

Elizabeth laughed. So that was it! Jessica had recently won a local beauty pageant, one Elizabeth had tried to stop. Elizabeth believed that beauty pageants were sexist, dated, and fundamentally unfair, and had argued that beauty queens weren't selected for their talents or intelligence, but on the basis of their appearance only. Once she'd participated in the pageant herself, Jessica had grudgingly conceded that her twin was right. Elizabeth was glad Jessica wasn't one hundred percent thrilled with her title. The lesson she'd learned might not have been easy, but it was very important.

But she did feel bad about Jessica and Frazer. One of the reasons her sister had entered the beauty pageant was to get the attention of Frazer. McConnell, one of her brother Steven's friends from college. She had gotten his attention, all right, but after two dates, it was clear their match was not made in heaven.

"Listen, forget about Frazer. I have an invitation to pass on to you," Elizabeth said. Jessica listened as Elizabeth described the barbecue at Roger Barrett-Patman's house on Friday night.

"Annie Whitman? What's she doing on the list? Is she going out with Tony Esteban now?" Jessica asked curiously. Annie was on the cheerleading squad with her, and it clearly pained her to hear new gossip through the most unlikely source—her twin sister. "Well, I can't go, anyway," she added before Elizabeth could answer her question about Annie and Tony. "I have to go to a stupid store opening downtown and cut a stupid ribbon. If you ask me, Miss Teen Sweet Valley is overworked."

"Maybe you can resign," Elizabeth suggested.

Jessica gave her a murderous look. "I'm not resigning," she said. "I've got to ask Robin and Amy if they know anything about Annie Whitman and Tony Esteban," she added.

Jessica's aquamarine eyes were intent, and Elizabeth knew that her sister would soon root out whatever was going on between Tony and Annie.

And to think I'm the one who wants to be a reporter, Elizabeth thought with a rueful smile. *Jessica is the real snoop in this house!*

Two

On Friday night Elizabeth and Todd drove over to the Patmans' house for Roger's barbecue. Though Todd seemed to be in a good mood Elizabeth couldn't help but wonder if he was still upset about her having accepted Roger's invitation. She would have to try extra hard to remind Todd that they could still be in love even in a crowded room.

"This place blows me away every time I see it," Todd said as he turned off the motor of his BMW and looked up at the awe-inspiring facade of the Patmans' mansion.

Nestled in a hillside overlooking the valley, the Patmans' huge home was replete with signs of luxury and wealth, including a tennis court just below the house and outbuildings that flanked the exquisite swimming pool. The estate looked very much like a movie set.

Todd rang the doorbell, and after a long pause Bruce opened the door. He gave them an arrogant smile. Bruce Patman easily managed to live up to the glamor surrounding him. "Liz and Todd," he drawled. "I guess you've come for our 'rescue a hoodlum' barbecue." He laughed. "Roger's out back with the little fiend. But I warn you, don't expect too much. You know what those people are like."

Elizabeth and Todd exchanged glances. Leave it to Bruce to reduce someone to a stereotype in seconds. Bruce was such a snob, Elizabeth thought angrily. Because of that, she herself had never thought him attractive, though she knew he was considered gorgeous by at least half the female population at school.

Luckily Roger came to the door to rescue them. "Hi! Come on out back. We'll be grilling some hot dogs and hamburgers in a few minutes," he said cheerfully.

"Gourmet choice, cousin," Bruce said snidely. He shook his head sorrowfully at Elizabeth and Todd. "I wanted something decent, like filet of salmon. But my cousin insisted on junk food. What can I say?" he continued obnoxiously. "You can take the boy out of the poorhouse, but you can't take the poorhouse out of the boy."

"Oh, cut it out, Bruce," Roger said in an offhand way. When Roger had first moved into the Patman estate his relationship with Bruce had been an extremely painful one. But as time

16

passed he'd learned how to handle his snobby cousin. Elizabeth had to chuckle at Roger's amused tolerance of Bruce.

Elizabeth and Todd followed the boys out onto the flagstone patio overlooking the Patmans' pool. Annie and Tony were there already, sitting at a table with a boy who Elizabeth guessed must be Mitch.

"Mitch, I've got two more friends for you to meet. This is Todd Wilkins and Elizabeth Wakefield," Roger said. "Mitch Ferguson," he added with a gesture at the boy. Mitch made no effort to get up and gave Elizabeth and Todd a once-over that was bordering on rude.

"Nice to meet you, Mitch," Elizabeth said.

"I'm only here 'cause I'm in trouble," Mitch replied with a challenging look at Elizabeth.

"Let me get you guys something to drink," Roger said quickly. "We've got lemonade and all kinds of soda."

Elizabeth took a seat after asking for some lemonade and looked at the threesome before her. She had to admit, Mitch *did* look a bit like a rough kid. But the effect was mostly due to his clothes and his haircut, Elizabeth thought, and neither could completely offset a certain fresh-faced boyishness about him. Mitch was wearing black jeans and a black T-shirt with the name of a rock group Elizabeth had never heard of emblazoned across it. One of his ears was pierced and he wore an expression that dared anyone to be nice to him.

17

Next to Mitch, Elizabeth thought, Tony and Annie looked particularly clean-cut. Tony was wearing a pair of faded blue jeans and a red polo shirt. His dark hair was still damp and freshly combed, and with his tanned, lean, muscular build, he looked the picture of the all-American athlete. Beside him, Annie's petite beauty was all the more striking. With her dark curly hair and green eyes, Annie was lovely to look at. The two were sitting close together, Elizabeth noticed, and Annie was hanging on every word Tony said. She wondered, as Jessica had, if the two were an item.

"Tony, are you ready for tomorrow?" Todd asked, taking a seat next to the hottest member of Sweet Valley High's track team.

Tony began to talk about the meet against Big Mesa, and Elizabeth excused herself to help Roger with the drinks.

"How's it going so far with Mitch?" she asked curiously.

"Mixed. My aunt and Bruce aren't exactly thrilled with him." Roger grinned. "He tried to tape up some rock posters in the guest room, the one loaded with antiques, and my aunt threw a fit. And Bruce thinks Mitch is just too low for words. Uncle Henry's much better about the situation. He thinks Mitch just needs a little straightening out, that he's basically a good kid. And that's what I think, too."

Elizabeth nodded as she helped Roger set

glasses on a tray. "Is he interested in sports at all?" she asked.

"Nope. He thinks sports are stupid. Or so he says. All he cares about is music. And I have to say, he's got the strangest taste of any kid I've ever met!"

Elizabeth laughed and the two went back to the table with the drinks. Tony was describing a set of workouts the coach had prescribed, and Elizabeth noticed that though Mitch was pretending to examine his fingers, he seemed to be listening.

Bruce yawned. "Aren't we going to talk about anything besides track? You runners are so obsessive."

Roger and Tony ignored the jibe. "The one I'm worried about tomorrow is Dean Maddingly," Tony continued, sitting forward a little. "He's a strong sprinter. I may have to face off against him in the 220, and he's going to be tough to beat."

Mitch looked up with something approaching interest.

"But I'm going to get him. I'm psyching him out," Tony continued. Mitch looked away, but Elizabeth had the impression he was still paying attention.

Bruce pushed back his chair. "I can't stand this. Call me when the food's ready," he said, strolling back into the house. Everyone laughed, and even Mitch looked a little less menacing.

"Come on, Annie. Let's start making some

burgers," Elizabeth said as she pushed back her chair. "It doesn't look as if we're ever going to get these guys to stop talking track!"

Annie seemed a little shy to Elizabeth that night. She didn't talk very much as they prepared the hamburgers for grilling. She seemed more interested in overhearing whatever Tony was talking about.

"Hey," Elizabeth said quietly. "Have you and Tony been seeing each other?"

Elizabeth's question brought a blush to Annie's face. "The relationship is pretty new," she whispered. "I guess I'm a little nervous. Tony and I have never been out in public before. Isn't that silly?" she asked shyly, pushing back her dark mop of hair.

"No," Elizabeth said, smiling. "It sounds normal to me."

Annie took a deep breath. "It's just, well, I like him so much!" she whispered. "I've never met a guy I cared about half as much as I care about Tony. You know I was seeing Charlie Markus, right? Well, he and I broke up a little while ago. I've been wary around guys since then, but Tony's different. He's a lot of fun. He's been great to me." Annie shrugged. "So even though I didn't intend to get serious so soon, I don't feel like being with anyone else but him."

"Annie, that's great!" Elizabeth said. "You seem to make a wonderful couple."

"At first I was also a little worried about getting involved with him right at the beginning of track season. Tony's got so much riding on this season," Annie said. "But he seems pretty normal about it. Not like some guys, who act as if the rest of the world has to stop just because they've started their season."

"Todd and I were talking about Tony on the way over here tonight," Elizabeth remarked. "Tony seems to be a very well-rounded person." She glanced back at the table, where Mitch was interrupting Tony's story with a rudely timed yawn. "Looks as if Roger's guest isn't very polite," she said with a smile.

Annie followed her glance and started to laugh. "I wouldn't worry about Tony. He's good with kids, especially boys. He'll keep him in line."

And that seemed to be the case. Tony didn't ignore Mitch's behavior, but he didn't make excuses for it, either. "Cut it out, Mitch. I'm telling a story," he said. And to Elizabeth's surprise, Mitch sat up straighter and stopped his phony yawning. When he next caught Tony's eye, Mitch's face wore an expression of grudging respect.

"Hey, did you have a good time tonight?" Tony asked on the way home.

Annie was sitting next to him in the used Mazda he'd bought the year before. She smelled so nice, Tony thought appreciatively. He didn't

21

know if it was perfume or the shampoo she used, but the scent was clean and pretty. It made him feel good.

"Yeah. I had a lot of fun. I like Roger, and Todd and Elizabeth." Annie giggled. "But Mitch's manners need a little polishing."

"Yeah, I hope Roger can help Mitch," Tony said. "Did you hear what he said when I asked him to come to the meet tomorrow? He told me that running was stupid." Tony laughed. "He couldn't have been ruder if he'd tried."

"Maybe *you* can help him, Tony," Annie said suddenly. "He responded quickly enough when you told him off for that phony yawning. I don't know if Roger will be firm enough with him."

Tony was surprised. "You think *I* can help him?"

"Why not? I think you're a great role model," Annie said lightly.

"Yeah, right," Tony teased her. "If he follows my lead, Mitch will end up spending his life running in circles!"

Annie laughed, and Tony looked over at her. He was having such a good time with her, he didn't want the evening to end. He pulled his car up in front of the apartment building where Annie lived with her mother. "Want me to walk you upstairs?" he asked softly.

Annie hesitated. "No," she said. "My mom and her boyfriend will be home. And I know *you've* got to get to bed early!"

"Actually, I have to stop by the gym before I go home," Tony admitted. "I left my stopwatch in my locker and I need it to time myself doing some sprints before the meet tomorrow."

"Tony—" Annie began.

Tony stopped her by sliding his hand under her chin and tipping her face up so he could look down into her lovely green eyes. "Annie, you're so beautiful." Tony couldn't believe he'd said what he'd just said.

Annie lowered her eyes.

"I mean . . ." Tony's voice trailed off and he felt butterflies in his stomach. This was a lot harder than running a race. How on earth did you ever figure out how to talk to a girl? Was there some kind of book you could read? Tony took a deep breath. "I just like you a lot, that's all," he said in a rush.

Annie parted her lips as if she were going to say something. But she didn't. She pulled his head down so his face was close to hers. "Tony, I like you, too. A lot," she finally whispered. And before Tony knew what was happening, Annie brushed his lips with hers. It was their first kiss. And she'd been the one to initiate it. Maybe some guys wouldn't have liked that, but Tony did. He liked Annie's independence, and her warmth. And he liked her kiss. His heart began to pound.

"Good night," she whispered. "I'll be at the meet tomorrow, OK? And I'll see you afterward."

Before Tony could answer she was gone.

Wow, Tony thought as he sat waiting until he saw that Annie had gotten safely inside the apartment building. He'd had no idea a girl could have so strong an impact on him. When he'd asked Annie to see a movie with him a few weeks before, he hadn't really figured much would come of it. And now, three weeks later, he found himself really hooked.

As he drove to the gym, Tony couldn't imagine how he could possibly feel better. The track season had just started and already it looked as if it was going to be his best ever, the one that might make his entire career. And he'd met a girl he really liked. What more could a guy want?

It was ten o'clock when Tony got to the gym. The locker room was almost empty, and just a few die-hards were still working out in the weight rooms. The gym was open until eleven o'clock on Friday and Saturday nights, and some guys were so obsessed about working out that they would stay until the guards kicked them out.

Tony had joined the gym the year before at his father's suggestion. Coach Featherston didn't think high-school athletes needed extra work-out time at a gym, but Tony's father had different ideas about training.

Joe Esteban had almost been a professional

football player. When he had been a teenager in San Diego, it was clear to anyone who watched him play that he had a great career in football ahead of him. When he had gotten to college, he continued to play ball and his career looked even more promising. Then Joe's mother had taken ill and he had to drop out of school and work to help pay her medical bills. Joe Esteban had never finished his degree, and he lost his chance at the pros.

In raising Tony, Mr. Esteban had made sports a priority. He'd tried his hardest to give his son every opportunity. Membership in this upscale gym was just one of the extras Mr. Esteban worked overtime to provide.

Until his junior year at Sweet Valley High, Tony had loved the support and attention his father gave him. In fact, until recently he'd never once questioned his father's involvement in his life. But now that track season was under way again, things were different at home. Tenser. At least three times a day his father asked him how practice had gone. What his times had been. Whether the talent scouts had been out to see him. Tony sighed, threw his duffel bag over his shoulder, and headed for the gym door. He was afraid his father was changing, becoming almost obsessed with his son's performance.

Tony pushed open the glass door and stepped inside. Instantly, his worries about his father seemed to fall away. It was good coming to the gym. Tony liked its atmosphere of friendly competitiveness. In the last few months he'd gotten to know a few older guys, most of them freshmen at the local community college, who spent most of their time in the weight rooms. Tony liked bantering with them.

Lou Orton was the guy from that crowd that Tony knew best. Lou was at the gym when Tony came in, working out on the bench press. Tony stopped to say hello to him after he'd retrieved his stopwatch.

"Hey, Esteban! Ready to wipe out Big Mesa tomorrow?" Lou asked him. He was wearing his customary workout clothes: a black tank top and a pair of black shorts.

"Yeah, I'm ready," Tony said. He looked enviously at Lou's muscular physique. "How much are you pressing these days?" Lou, who was eighteen, was a wrestler with national medals to his name.

"Three-sixty," Lou said with a grin.

"Three hundred and sixty pounds? Jeez, what are you doing to yourself?" Tony exclaimed. As a runner, it was hard for him to believe that a person could pump up that big. It was one thing to add a little speed, but a completely different thing to bench-press that much weight.

"You runners don't know a thing about muscle," Lou teased him. "Let me get you on the mats some day and I'll show you a real sport."

Tony laughed. He liked talking to Lou, but

sometimes he didn't know how seriously to take him. "Yeah, right. Come on out to the meet tomorrow and *I'll* show *you* a real sport."

"Maybe I will," Lou drawled. "Listen, you leaving now? You want to head over to the Beach Disco and see what's happening?"

"No, thanks. I've got to get some sleep. I'm facing someone tough tomorrow in the 220," Tony said.

Even if he had not needed to go home, Tony wasn't sure he would have gone to the Beach Disco with Lou. He liked Lou around the gym. But sometimes he had the feeling that . . . He couldn't quite put it into words, but there was something about Lou Orton and some of his friends that bugged him.

I'm getting paranoid, Tony told himself after he'd said good night to Lou and headed out to the parking lot. Lou was a good-enough guy. And if he liked to spend half his waking hours pumping iron, what was wrong with that?

Both he and Lou were athletes. To Tony, being serious about a sport, whatever it was, was all-important. Not only was Lou serious about wrestling, he had taken a strong interest in Tony's track career. No doubt about it. Lou was a guy you could admire.

I really should be flattered, Tony thought as he got into his car. Lou was a big deal around the gym. There were a lot of other guys Lou didn't even notice.

Tony pulled out of the parking lot. He knew

his father would be waiting up for him. He'd want to talk strategy for the next day's meet.

Lately, Tony thought a bit irritably, *it's like Dad's running the races instead of me*. And then a wave of guilt washed over him. What kind of son was he not to appreciate all his father had sacrificed for him?

Three

"OK, Annie Whitman," Jessica said. She put her hands on her hips and faced her friend. "Since when do you hold out on your fellow cheerleaders? You haven't even mentioned the fact that you've been going out with the star of the track team!"

Annie blushed beet-red. It was Saturday morning and some of the cheerleaders had met to watch the meet together. Of the seven girls on the squad, only Robin Wilson, Annie's best friend, knew anything about her relationship with Tony. And at this early stage Annie didn't feel at all ready for a public discussion of her feelings. How had Jessica found out she and Tony were dating? Then she realized that Elizabeth must have told her sister after the barbecue the night before.

"Jessica, maybe Annie doesn't want to talk about it," Robin said pointedly.

"Why not? You're nuts, Annie," Amy Sutton cried. "If I were going out with Tony, I'd brag about it to *everyone!*"

Jessica giggled. "Yeah, but that's you, Amy." Amy Sutton had a reputation for being boy crazy, although lately she had been dating Barry Rork, a senior, fairly steadily.

"I mean it. Tony's adorable," Amy protested.

Annie looked from one girl to the next. She still felt strangely shy about Tony. But it was flattering having the other girls so interested. "Our relationship is brand-new," she admitted at last. "I haven't said anything because it doesn't feel like there's anything to say yet. We're really just good friends," she added helplessly.

Jessica looked slyly at her friends. "You can tell she's in love. Whenever a girl says 'we're just friends' with that gaga look in her eyes, you know for sure. Don't fight it, Annie!"

Annie wished she felt sure enough about her relationship with Tony to accept her friends' banter. She was a little afraid that if she talked about her feelings too openly, the whole romance would vanish into thin air, like a burst bubble.

Jessica and Amy began to discuss the celebration party they were planning for the track team that evening. "I think the Beach Disco is the right place," Jessica said. "Dana Larson told me The Droids are playing there tonight." Dana was the lead singer of The Droids, Sweet Valley High's own rock group.

Annie was glad the others were so certain that Sweet Valley High was going to win the meet. She herself was a tiny bit nervous about the outcome. Annie knew Tony was anxious about the meet, too. From what he'd told her, she knew his father was putting a lot of pressure on him. "How can you guys be so positive we're going to win? Big Mesa's got a strong team," Annie said.

Jessica grinned and looked at Amy. "The girlfriends always worry," she remarked. Both girls burst out laughing. Annie bit her lip and looked out onto the field where the coaches were setting up the markers for the first race. They were right. She *was* worrying too much. Big Mesa was good, but Sweet Valley was better. And by that evening she'd be celebrating Tony's first big win of the season.

"I love track meets," Winston Egbert announced. "But why do they have to use that stupid gun to start each race? If I were out there on the field, I'd be so busy worrying about whether or not I'd gotten shot that I'd forget to start running."

Everyone laughed. Winston was the unofficial clown of the junior class, and he had a way of holding a captive audience.

Elizabeth was glad they'd gotten to the meet early enough so that everyone could sit together. Todd sat on her left, and Enid Rollins, her best friend, on her right. Winston sat in the row below them with Claire Middleton and Dana Larson; behind them sat Tom McKay and Amy's boyfriend, Barry, two good friends who were on the tennis team. It was a beautiful, sunny morning, and the crowd was in high spirits. Everyone, that is, but Todd. He didn't join in any of the conversation around him, and his eyes were focused on the track. Just before the meet began, Enid leaned over and asked Elizabeth if everything was OK with him.

"I think so. I'll tell you later," Elizabeth whispered back.

"Track's a great sport to watch," John Pfiefer said appreciatively. "I like the sprinting the best."

"Hey, look over there," Tom said, pointing down to the coach's table. "See that guy in the red cap? That's Burr Davidson."

"Who's he?" Elizabeth asked.

"He's a big talent scout. He targets a lot of players for college drafts, pre-Olympic teams, that sort of thing," Todd explained.

Elizabeth's eyes widened. "Do you think he's here to watch Tony?"

Winston nodded. "Yeah, and he won't be the only one. By the end of the season, Tony'll probably have lots of offers."

"Especially if he wins in the All-County," Todd reminded them.

Elizabeth settled back to watch the meet. Even though she wasn't covering it for *The Oracle*, she'd brought a notebook and pen with her to take some notes to familiarize herself with the events. Though she hadn't been to very many track meets, she found herself enjoying this one. Tony won his first event easily, and forty-five minutes into the meet Sweet Valley was leading Big Mesa by a comfortable margin.

"The 220 is next," Todd said, sitting forward. "Tony's going to have a hard time with that guy in the far lane. He's really good."

"Yeah. What's his name? Maddingly, I think. I've heard about him," Tom commented. "But Tony'll take care of him!"

All eyes were on Tony as he trotted up to the starting line, loosening his shoulders and shaking out his arms and legs. The runners crouched on the tarmac and waited for the starting signal. An expectant hush fell over the crowd, the gun was fired, and the boys were off.

Elizabeth kept her eyes glued on Tony. The muscles in his lean legs rippled as he ran. He pulled himself ahead of Dean Maddingly. He was almost at the finish line when a gasp came from the frontmost section of the bleachers. Elizabeth and her friends automatically stood up and, on the sidelines, Annie Whitman grabbed hold of Jessica's arm.

In a split second, Tony had stumbled, clutched wildly at the air around him, and fallen on the track. Now he lay still on the ground. Coach Featherston raced out to him, followed by other members of the Sweet Valley High team, and Annie.

"Tony, what happened?" the coach said as he crouched beside him.

Tony seemed unable to unclench his jaw. "It's my right knee," he gasped. "Feels like I pulled something pretty badly."

"Dan, call an ambulance," the coach said to his assistant.

Tony struggled to sit up. "I don't need an ambulance," he said tightly. "I'll be fine. I just need to catch my breath. I—" The effort of moving made him fall back helplessly. The coach nodded to his assistant. "Go ahead, call 911. We need to get him to the hospital. Tony, do you think you can stand if we help you?" the coach continued.

Tony shook his head. "I can't believe it. What happened to me? How could I have tripped like that?" Tony's voice was filled with anguish. "Coach, I've never done that in my whole life. I just tripped, on *nothing*."

"Tony, it happens. Just take it easy. What matters is making sure your knee's OK," Coach Featherston replied.

But Tony couldn't stay quiet. "Burr Davidson is here. He saw it all," he groaned. "God, I really messed up!"

34

"Even top athletes sometimes take a spill," Coach Featherston said calmly.

Just then Mr. Esteban pushed to the front of the crowd surrounding Tony. "Tony, are you OK?" he asked. Then, in an almost accusatory tone, he added, "What happened out there?"

Tony had to gasp for another breath before responding. "I don't know, Dad. I guess I really blew it."

Mr. Esteban pulled Coach Featherston aside. "This fall isn't going to hurt Tony's season, is it?" he asked.

Coach Featherston raised his eyebrows. "Why don't we just see what kind of injury Tony's sustained before we jump to any conclusions?" he said. Mr. Esteban nodded tensely. While they waited for the ambulance he paced back and forth, occasionally barking anxious instructions to no one in particular.

Coach Featherston had a blanket brought out to cover Tony's lower body. "I want you to lie still and breathe deeply. Until we get this knee looked at, I don't want you trying to move yourself again. Do you understand?"

Tony nodded weakly. It felt like a long time before the first cries of the ambulance's siren were audible. Until then Annie had stood away from the coach and the other team members closely surrounding Tony. Now she pushed forward and watched as the paramedics began to prepare a stretcher.

"OK, folks, we need you to back away," one of the paramedics instructed.

"Yes, back away," Mr. Esteban echoed, making shooing motions to clear a path for the stretcher. He stepped right in front of Annie, blocking her view of Tony until the ambulance doors were closed behind him.

Tony was taken to the emergency room at Joshua Fowler Memorial Hospital. Annie made sure she got to the hospital as soon as she could. She wasn't the only one who'd come to see Tony. The waiting room was crowded with friends and well-wishers. Even Coach Featherston was there. Annie was dying to see Tony alone.

To her relief, Mrs. Esteban called her out of the waiting room. "Tony's seeing his doctor right now. He wants you to come in so he can have a few minutes with you alone," Mrs. Esteban told her with a reassuring smile.

"How is he?" Annie asked anxiously.

"I think he's going to be just fine." Mrs. Esteban sighed. "We've had a bad scare, but the doctor said there's no sign of permanent damage. He tore a tendon in his knee, that's all."

Annie breathed a sigh of relief. Only now, hearing the good news, did she realize how alarmed she had been. Annie followed Mrs. Esteban into the examination room. Tony was

36

sitting up in the bed, listening earnestly to the doctor seated in a chair beside him. Both looked up when Annie came into the room. So did Mr. Esteban, who was pacing nervously by the far side of the bed as the doctor spoke.

"Annie, hi," Tony said.

"I'm so glad you're all right," Annie replied fervently. She walked over to the side of his bed and took his hand.

"Dr. Griffin, this is my, uh, friend, Annie Whitman. Annie, this is Dr. Griffin." Tony looked at his parents. "You remember Annie. She came over to the house a few weeks ago."

"Of course we do," Mrs. Esteban said warmly.

Mr. Esteban didn't acknowledge his son's introduction. "You were talking about that knee," he reminded the doctor. Annie thought Mr. Esteban referred to Tony's leg as if it existed apart from Tony himself.

The doctor nodded. "Yes, I was." He looked at Tony. "As I was saying, you're lucky. You shouldn't run into any serious complications, as long as you make sure you stay off that leg for the next week. And I mean *off*, completely. You'll need to pick up some crutches on the way home from the hospital."

"Crutches!" Tony cried. "But—"

Dr. Griffin put up his hand. "Absolutely no weight on that leg for one week. I want you to keep ice on the knee tonight to reduce the swelling. You may feel some pain for a day or two, so I'll give you some painkillers just in case. In a week come see me in my office and we'll take another look. And in the meantime I also want you to take something to reduce any further inflammation of the muscles. I'm prescribing some cortisone pills you should take each day until you see me again next week."

"Dr. Griffin, I've got important track meets coming up—" Tony began.

"Yes," Mr. Esteban cut in. "This is a crucial season for Tony. He's got talent scouts coming to see him each week. He can't wait forever for this thing to heal."

Mrs. Esteban frowned. "Darling, listen to what the doctor's saying. Tony can't rush right back to track practice. He's got to give the injury time to heal properly."

Dr. Griffin got to his feet. "Let's hope you'll be ready for track soon, Tony. But remember, you're a human being, not a machine, and your knee will heal in its own time. Be patient and be careful. I expect to see a big improvement in the next week or two." Dr. Griffin pulled a slip of paper from his pocket and handed it to Tony. "I've written down the name of an excellent physiotherapist who works at the hospital's outpatient clinic. You should check in with her today, and start seeing her as soon as you feel ready. She'll be able to recommend some exercises that will help you regain strength in that leg. If you're still experiencing pain after a month or so, we may have to consider cortisone injections, maybe even microscopic surgery.

But for now let's take the most conservative approach. You're young and healthy, and there's no reason you shouldn't heal quickly."

"Doctor, a word with you, please," Mr. Esteban said as he followed the doctor out of the room. Mrs. Esteban gave her son a quick kiss and followed them.

Tony waited until they'd left the room before turning to Annie. "Listen to that," he said bitterly. " 'If you're still experiencing pain after a month.' A month! Annie, the All-County meet is only seven weeks away! I can't wait a whole month for my knee to get better!"

"He didn't really say it *would* take a month," Annie pointed out.

But Tony seemed not to have heard her. "This is crazy," he said woefully as he stared down at his bandaged right knee. Then he looked up at Annie. "You heard my dad. You saw how important it is for him that I get better. He's got as much riding on this track season as I do. Maybe even more."

"You'll be better in no time. Wait and see," Annie said hopefully.

"I'd better be," Tony said. "Annie, my whole career is at stake. If my leg doesn't heal fast, I'm completely ruined!" Tony's dark eyes were filled with fear. "*I* could stand it, I really could. But what I couldn't stand would be watching my dad's dream just die. For his sake, as well as mine, I've got to get better—fast."

Four

After a good night's sleep, Tony was feeling better enough to hate being on crutches. "These things are ridiculous. My knee doesn't even hurt that badly anymore," he complained to his parents as he practiced walking around the living room Sunday morning.

"I'm glad you're feeling better, Tony. But you heard what Dr. Griffin said. You're to stay completely off that leg for at least a week," his mother said sternly.

Tony sighed heavily. "I think it's stupid. My leg would get better more quickly if I could walk around on it."

Mr. Esteban looked at his son anxiously. "I have to agree with your mother this time, Tony. You heard what the doctor said. If you don't stay off your leg, we could *really* be in trouble!"

Tony grimaced. He knew when to push his parents and when not to. It was clear he wasn't going to get much support from them if he didn't do everything Dr. Griffin had ordered.

Tony might hate having to use the crutches, but he was very interested in the physical therapy exercises the hospital physiotherapist, Suzanne Rochester, had shown him before he left the hospital Saturday evening. They weren't terribly strenuous, but at least they made him feel as if he was actively on his way to recovery.

Tony had gone over his fall a dozen times in his head. What made him trip? One minute he'd been running with all his might, and the next minute he'd had the sickening sense of falling. Then there'd been the searing pain in his knee, followed by complete confusion. Tony had never been injured before, not once in his entire high school career!

He'd gotten a lot of attention since the accident. There had been phone calls from some of the guys on the team, from Coach Featherston, and from Coach Schultz, Sweet Valley High's athletic director. Annie had been very sweet. She'd brought over some funny little presents to divert him. Mrs. Esteban was planning his favorite dinner. And at lunchtime Roger stopped by to see how he was feeling.

"What happened at the meet after I got hurt?" Tony asked Roger. "Did we win, or was it a forfeit?"

"We won. And we'll be competing against

Big Mesa again later in the season. You'll have your chance to beat them, then," Roger said encouragingly. Then he went on to tell Tony that the victory party the cheerleaders had planned had been postponed until he could attend. It was nice to know that his friends and classmates were worried about him, but the novelty of being injured and of receiving lots of special attention was wearing off. Tony was already sick of being an invalid.

Tony was sitting in his father's armchair with his injured leg propped up on a hassock. He wiggled his toes and sighed. How long would it be before he was ready to run again? Was he going to spend the next two months on the sidelines?

As if reading his mind, Roger got up and clapped him on the shoulder. "Hurry up and get better, guy. We need you out there."

Before Tony could tell him that he fully intended to, Roger snapped his fingers. "Oh, I almost forgot. I have something for you from Mitch." He reached into his pocket and took out a small, clumsily wrapped package.

It was a cassette of some rock group neither Roger nor Tony had ever heard of. On the package were scribbled the words, "Tony, sorry you hurt your leg. Get better soon."

Tony grinned. "That was nice of him," he said. He was surprised. Mitch hadn't seemed overly impressed with him at the barbecue two nights before. The present was a pretty thoughtful gesture from such a tough kid!

"Don't look too happy," Roger joked. "If it's anything like the music he's been playing at top volume in our house, you'll play it once and decide you've had enough of recuperating. Mitch doesn't exactly have *restful* taste in music!"

After Roger had gone Tony clumped around the living room on the crutches, just to keep from getting bored.

"Mom," he asked at about three o'clock, "if I call the physiotherapist and she says it's OK, do you think I could go over to the gym and use the whirlpool?"

His mother put down the book she was reading and looked at her son. "Poor Tony. You're really feeling cooped up, aren't you?"

He nodded. "If I could just get out of the house, I think I'd feel a lot better."

"OK. Check with the physiotherapist and make sure it's all right," his mother replied.

Tony was delighted. A quick phone call to Suzanne Rochester confirmed that the whirlpool would be excellent therapy for his knee.

Tony actually got a kick out of showing up at the gym on crutches. A bunch of the guys had heard about his accident. It was almost a hero's welcome.

"Hey, that's a drag. An injury during the first big meet of the season," Lou said as he draped an arm over Tony's shoulder. "What happened to you? You think any of the guys you were racing against tried to trip you?"

"No way," Tony said. He shook his head. "I just fell. I don't know how." Tony described his going to the hospital in the ambulance, his being examined, and finally, his seeing the physiotherapist. He tried to make the story just a bit more colorful than it actually had been in order to keep Lou's attention.

"What a drag," Lou repeated. "How long do you have to use those things?" he added, indicating the crutches with a jerk of his head.

"A week," Tony said. "But in a few days I'm going to start swimming and lifting weights so I don't get too badly out of shape."

One of Lou's friends, Randy Olson, joined the two boys. "Lou, you should give him some of your *magic vitamins*," he said with a wink. "A week or two on those and he won't feel *any* pain."

"What do you mean, 'magic vitamins'?" Tony asked. Lou frowned and snapped his towel at Randy. "Get lost, Olson," he said gruffly. "Nothing," he added to Tony. "Just some stuff a couple of the other wrestlers and I take to help us beef up a little." He watched Randy walk off. "Randy, for instance. He's wrestling in the one-hundred-ninety pound class. Last year he was in the one-hundred-seventy-seven pound class."

"Wow," Tony said. He was impressed. "I didn't know there were vitamins that could do that." Then he looked carefully at Lou. Was he teasing, or was he being serious?

"Yeah, they're not exactly vitamins," Lou said with a shrug. "But let me know if you want to try them, especially if that knee isn't healing fast enough. OK? You could give them a try, see if they help."

Tony shrugged. "I don't know. The doctor gave me some pills. I should be back at practice soon," he said with more confidence than he felt. If Tony had his way, he'd be back in a day or two. His knee was still sore, but he knew the pain wouldn't last. Not if he didn't let it.

"Want to come watch me work out for a while?" Lou grinned. "I can tell you some more about those magic vitamins."

Tony laughed off Lou's offer, but he couldn't help but feel a surge of curiosity. "Nah," he said. "I'm going to sit in the whirlpool for a while. Get some of the soreness out of my leg."

Lou shrugged. "Hey, do it your way. But if you change your mind, let me know."

Tony watched Lou saunter off to the weight room. The guy sure knew how to bulk up, that was for sure. Well, it was good to know Lou was around if he needed him. If he didn't see a big improvement in his knee right away, Tony would ask Lou's advice. Track season only came around once a year. And this season was far too valuable for Tony to waste on the sidelines.

*　*　*

On Monday Annie and Tony ate lunch together outside. It took Tony several tries before he was able to balance his crutches against the picnic table. "Stupid things," he said angrily. "I can't wait to get rid of them!"

"I don't know," Annie said with a grin. "They make you look kind of heroic."

Tony ignored her teasing. "You've been great," he said as he pushed his food from one side of his plate to the other. "Everyone has been."

"Tony, are you all right?" Annie asked gently.

"Yeah, I'm fine. I'm just kind of worried, that's all. My knee doesn't feel any better today than it did yesterday. I called Dr. Griffin this morning to ask him about the pills he prescribed for me. Do you know they're only an anti-inflammatory painkiller, not much different from aspirin?"

"That makes sense, doesn't it?" Annie said. "You probably don't need anything stronger."

Tony frowned. "It's just that a lot's riding on this season for me, Annie. I got a call yesterday from Burr Davidson, the talent scout who was out watching on Saturday. He was really sympathetic about what happened, but he wanted to know when he'd be able to watch me run again. I didn't know what to tell him."

Annie took a bite of her sandwich. Tony

seemed overly anxious about his injury. He'd talked about little else since it happened.

"I'm sure the doctor knew what he was talking about," she said after a minute. "It won't be all that long before you're one hundred percent again."

"I don't *have* all that long," Tony answered almost angrily. He stretched out his leg and looked down at it accusingly.

"Tony . . ." Annie reached out and put her hand on his arm. "You've got to give yourself a break. It's only been a couple of days since the accident."

Tony nodded toward the crutches. "I hate those things," he said. "I hate having to miss practice. Do you have any idea how hard it's going to be to get back in shape if I have to sit out much longer?"

"But you'll be able to start swimming soon," Annie pointed out. "That'll help."

Tony sighed. "I guess so. Annie, I'm sorry. I don't mean to complain. You must think I sound like a broken record. I'm just disappointed and frustrated, that's all. And another thing—" He frowned, then shook his head. "Never mind." When Annie raised her eyebrows, Tony sat back in his chair. "My dad's been having a hard time accepting this, too. I think he's even more worried about my knee than I am. I can't help but feel *guilty*, as if by getting hurt, I took something away from him."

"Tony, you didn't fall on purpose! Look, I

think you need to take your mind off the accident," Annie said. "I've got an idea. There's a new miniature golf course down by the marina. Why don't we round up some people after school and play a few games?"

Tony looked doubtfully at his crutches. "I'm not sure if—"

"Oh, come on," Annie said brightly. "You'll manage. I'm even willing to bet you'll beat me!"

Tony laughed. "OK. Why not. It's probably the only competition I'll be getting for a while!"

"What *is* this game?" Mitch asked. He glared at the club Todd handed to him. "We don't play this in the city. And I don't think I'm going to like it."

"Haven't you ever played miniature golf before?" Elizabeth asked.

"Uh-uh. It looks ridiculous," Mitch replied. He looked around the colorful course with an expression of scorn.

"It's not ridiculous. It's a lot of fun," Tony said. He grabbed a club and used one crutch to hop his way to the first tee. "It's even more fun if you can use both legs," he added.

Mitch watched him closely. "Well," he said after Tony fired off a hole in one, "I guess it might be all right." Then he added quickly, "But it might still be as stupid as it looks."

Tony and Roger moved away from Mitch to

let him take the next shot and went over to where Elizabeth was standing.

"I think Mitch responds to you," Roger said quietly to Tony. "He acts a bit different around you. Not as snide as he usually does. I get the feeling he respects you or something."

Tony laughed. "I don't know why. I'm always correcting or contradicting him." He shrugged. "Who knows? Maybe he likes it. At least he knows I'm listening to him." The two boys moved to a nearby bench and started to enter their scores on the scorecard.

Annie fell in beside Elizabeth. "I'm not much good at miniature golf," she said with a rueful smile. "I only suggested it because I was hoping it would cheer Tony up."

"Is he having a hard time dealing with the injury?" Elizabeth asked sympathetically.

"Boy, is he," Annie replied. "It's the first time he's ever been injured badly. He's very impatient with himself. In fact, I'm worried he may try to use his leg before the doctor says it's safe. If he does, he could *really* hurt himself and turn a minor injury into something very serious."

Elizabeth sighed. "I suppose it's the down side of having the kind of talent and dedication that Tony has."

Annie walked on to join Tony, and Elizabeth rejoined Todd at the next hole. "I thought we were going for a bike ride together this afternoon. You didn't tell me you were going to change our plans to involve four other people," Todd said tensely.

Elizabeth was surprised. "Todd, we didn't have definite plans. And when Annie asked me to join them, I just thought you would want to help cheer Tony up."

"Yeah, well, I don't mind helping out a friend, if we can also get some time to ourselves." Todd put his hand on Elizabeth's shoulder. "But lately, Liz, I never see you without at least ten other people between us!"

Elizabeth was about to answer when Tony stepped in between them. "Pardon me. The walking wounded one is up next."

"We can talk later," Elizabeth whispered apologetically.

"Yeah, right." Todd's voice was heavy with irony. "Maybe we can invite the whole junior class along to talk it over with us."

Elizabeth bit her lip. It was beginning to look like Todd's desire to spend time alone with her was much more serious than she'd imagined. But there wasn't much Elizabeth could do about it at the moment.

After a while it became clear that Mitch was going to win the first game. "Hey, this game isn't as stupid as it looked!" Mitch said in a voice bordering on enthusiastic. He tapped Tony on the shoulder with his club. "Thanks for the pointers," he said brusquely.

Tony smiled. "No problem, Mitch."

When Mitch had walked away Annie tucked

her arm through Tony's. "Looks like you won yourself a new friend, Tony. Mitch obviously thinks you're pretty cool." She gave him a quick kiss on the cheek. "And I happen to agree with him."

Five

Roger stopped by Tony's house on Friday evening. "Tony, I've got a big favor to ask you," he said when the two boys were alone together in the living room. "It's about Mitch."

"Sure, Roger. What's up?" Tony asked.

Roger took a deep breath. "Mitch is in trouble again. My aunt found an empty beer bottle in his bedroom and she wants to send him back to his mother. I convinced her to let him stay, but this is his last chance. I could try talking to him, but I'm not sure he'd listen to me the way he seems to listen to you. Someone's got to straighten him out, and fast!"

"Mitch was drinking in your house?"

"I guess so. It was only one bottle of beer, and I don't really agree with my aunt that it's cause to send him home." Roger sighed. "But my uncle's going along with her. And I'm concerned about Mitch. He needs to understand how easy it is to go from sneaking a couple of beers to having a real drinking problem."

Tony nodded. "Yeah. Mitch is only thirteen, right? How could he have gotten the beer?"

"You've got me." Roger shrugged. "I'd hate to have to call Denise and tell her I can't help her son. But Mitch doesn't listen to me. The only one he seems to look up to is you."

"Why don't you let me take him to the track meet Saturday?" Tony suggested after a moment. "We can watch you guys run, and I can play big brother to him."

"Thanks, Tony," Roger said gratefully. "I think going to a track meet is a good idea. Probably one of the reasons Mitch admires you is because you're so dedicated to your sport."

Tony shook his head. "Who's dedicated these days? Given the rate at which my knee is healing, I don't think I can claim to be dedicated to anything other than warming the bench!"

"Come on, Tony. You'll be back on the track before you know it," Roger said.

"Yeah, sure," Tony said skeptically. "Listen, try not to worry about Mitch. I'll give him a stern talking-to." He grinned. "I'll pretend I'm Coach Featherston giving the annual Your Body Is a Temple lecture!"

When Roger had gone Tony sat alone and thought about his situation. Saturday the Sweet Valley High track team would square off against the Palisades Pumas. How much longer would it be before he could go back to practice, and how much longer before he was ready to run a race again? What was supposed to be his career-making season was off to a dismal start.

"I don't get it," Mitch said to Tony on Saturday afternoon. "What's the point? All these guys line up and run around in a circle. What do they get out of it, anyway?"

"I don't know why other people do it. But for me, running's the best thing in the world," Tony said. He knew Mitch was really listening to him. Tony figured it was partly because he didn't talk down to Mitch. He took his questions seriously and answered him as if they were equals. "Running a good race is one of the most satisfying things I know. You feel your whole body's pulling together for the same goal."

Mitch's expression was thoughtful. "I can't really imagine it," he said after a long pause. "I'm a lousy runner. I'm the worst in my school."

Tony shrugged. "So maybe for you it'll be music, not sports. Everyone's got something they're really good at, something they really love. But I'll tell you one thing, Mitch. You've got to play fair in your own game. You may not always like the rules, but you've got to respect them." He squinted up at the sun, then looked

54

back down at Mitch. "You'd be surprised how many rules have good reasons behind them. Like not drinking."

Mitch turned red and stared down at his hands.

"Do you know how messed up you can get from drinking?" Tony cleared his throat. "I had a friend once, a guy I used to work out with. The year he got his learner's permit, his parents got divorced. It was a tough time for him, and he had a couple of buddies who were into drinking. One night he took his girlfriend out in the car, even though when you only have your permit you're not supposed to drive without an adult in the car with you."

"What happened?" Mitch asked.

"Well, he'd had a couple of beers before he left the house, and he got in an accident." Tony swallowed hard. He remembered all too well how horrible it had been. "Brian was fine, but his girlfriend was badly hurt. I don't think he'll ever forgive himself as long as he lives for what he did to her."

Mitch stared down at the ground. "Was she OK in the end? The girlfriend?" Mitch asked.

"Not OK. She got a little better, but she'll never be the same." Tony looked at Mitch. "I'll level with you. Roger told me about his aunt finding the beer bottle. He asked me to talk to you about it."

"Yeah, I figured," Mitch said. He looked

embarrassed and uncomfortable. "It wasn't a big deal. It was just one beer."

"It *is* a big deal for a couple of reasons. First, you're underage. You're only thirteen. It's illegal for you to buy alcohol or to drink it. Drinking for you is against the law. And that's really serious."

"Well, it's a dumb law, then," Mitch muttered.

"You may think so," Tony said mildly. "But like I said, there's usually a good reason behind a rule. And I'll tell you something else, Mitch. Drinking isn't going to solve whatever it is that's bugging you. You've got to figure out some other way to deal with it."

Mitch stared ahead at the field. "It's easy for you," he said thickly. "You've got it made. Your parents think you're the greatest, you're a big track star, you're probably going to turn out famous or something. It's a lot different for me. I'm just a nothing kid from L.A. I'm not good at sports, I'm not good at anything. My dad . . ."

Tony put his hand on Mitch's shoulder. He wished he could tell Mitch the truth, that right now Tony was disappointing his father and himself. That everything was *not* easy for him. But the last thing Mitch needed to hear was Tony's problems. "I think you're OK. Doesn't that count for anything?"

Mitch swiped at his eyes. "I dunno," he

said. "You don't really think that," he added accusingly.

"Listen, Mitch, do me a favor," Tony said. "I want you to cut out the drinking. Really cut it out. There's a clinic here in town that runs a counseling program called Project Youth. You can go there and talk to someone if you want to. But no more drinking. You promise me?"

"Yeah." Mitch took a deep breath. "I promise."

Tony put his hand out to shake. "OK," he said. For the first time since his accident the week before, Tony felt good. "We've got ourselves a deal."

Mitch's hand felt surprisingly small when they shook. *Only thirteen years old*, Tony thought.

"Hey, you've got your appointment with Dr. Griffin later, right?" Annie asked Tony after the track meet.

Tony nodded. He couldn't wait. Finally he'd be able to get off the crutches and back to practice! For the past day or two he hadn't noticed much pain in his knee, though the muscles in his leg still felt pretty weak.

"I've got to tell you, Annie," Tony said, "sitting on the bench watching Kyle Young lose both my events and seeing the Pumas run off with a win that should've been ours—well, it wasn't my idea of a fun morning."

"How about if I drive you to the doctor's? I

want to be there for the big uncrutching cere-mony," Annie suggested cheerfully.

"Sure!" Tony smiled. "I wouldn't want you to miss it. You've stayed by me through this long, lousy week." Tony squeezed her hand. "I know I haven't been much fun lately. I promise not to be half as much of an ogre once I get out on the field again."

"Don't expect too much of yourself at first, Tony. Remember, you've been off your leg all week. It may take a little while to get back in tiptop shape," Annie reminded him.

"No way," Tony said impatiently. "I'll be running in the next meet. I guarantee it."

Dr. Griffin stepped back from the examining table and patted Tony's shoulder. "You look fine. I'd even be willing to buy your crutches back from you," he teased.

Tony was flushed with excitement. "You mean it? I'm OK?"

Dr. Griffin looked at him thoughtfully. "Yes, you're fine. But you're not going to like what I'm about to say. You're going to feel a little tenderness in that knee for several weeks, pos-sibly longer. I don't see any reason why you can't start running again, but I don't want you to expect miracles. The body doesn't heal over-night."

Tony heard nothing other than the words, "I don't see any reason why you can't start running again." He was free! He had to restrain himself from jumping up and bolting out of the office.

Ice at night, take it easy, build up speed gradually, try not to overdo it . . . Tony barely listened to Dr. Griffin's recommendations. In his mind's eye he was out on the field, running. Burr Davidson and Coach Featherston were watching him and they were exulting over his progress. *We never thought he'd be out there again,* he imagined them saying. *And now here he is, an Olympic semi-finalist. . . .*

Dr. Griffin jolted Tony out of his reverie. "I can't rule out the possibility that we might have to consider those cortisone injections in a few weeks if the swelling is not completely gone. Call me if you experience any abnormal discomfort. OK?"

Tony nodded, but he knew he wouldn't be back to see Dr. Griffin. His knee would be fine. Tony joined Annie in the waiting room and gave her a huge bear hug. He was so ecstatic, he almost didn't notice the dull pain in his knee. Almost.

"This is pathetic," Tony muttered.

It was Sunday afternoon and at Tony's insistence he and Roger were at the school track. Roger was timing Tony. So far the results were awful.

It wasn't so much that his knee hurt. That

59

was the wrong way to describe it. Tony felt as if he was running with a weight attached to his leg.

"Listen, take it easy. You can't expect to be back one hundred percent the first day," Roger said.

Tony wasn't at all reassured. "My times shouldn't be off this much. This is ridiculous."

"Maybe you shouldn't be running yet," Roger said uncertainly. "Didn't the doctor and the coaches say you should wait awhile before coming back to practice?"

Tony didn't answer. *Wait awhile. Wait awhile.* He'd heard that phrase over and over again. Well, he was sick and tired of waiting. He knew he'd performed horribly. So much for his fantasies about Burr Davidson and the Olympics. So much about living up to his father's expectations. The All-County meet was less than six weeks away. At this rate, he'd be lucky if he even qualified to run in it.

Tony felt disgusted with himself. He didn't know what he was going to do, but he knew he had to do something—and fast.

Six

Tony had scheduled appointments with his physiotherapist, Suzanne Rochester, for Tuesdays and Thursdays after school. He couldn't wait to get to her office on Tuesday afternoon to tell her how dismally he'd performed on Sunday.

"So what's going on?" he asked when he'd told her everything. "This is supposed to be a minor injury. So why am I not seeing any big improvement?"

"You're too hard on yourself, Tony," Suzanne replied. "You've had an accident. Your body's still healing itself." She shook her head with a smile. "You athletes are terrible to work with," she joked. "Sometimes I think no one abuses their bodies more than you guys do."

"You should've seen my times," Tony repeated. "At this rate, I won't even be allowed

61

to stay on the team. Forget about scoring any major prizes."

Suzanne pointed to the examination table. "Get up there. Now, let's have a look," she said. Suzanne's expert fingers felt Tony's knee. "Yeah, still a little tender, I bet," she said. "Well, I'll give you a new set of exercises for this week. And some moral support. But otherwise, all you can do is be patient and wait for your body to heal itself."

Tony couldn't even meet her gaze. *Patient.* That word again.

"Don't lose heart," Suzanne said as Tony was leaving her office. "You're looking a lot better already. Remember, only a few days ago you came in here on crutches."

Tony nodded disconsolately. "Thanks, Suzanne. See you on Thursday."

Tony knew his father was eagerly waiting for him at home. He'd want to know how the appointment with the physiotherapist went. Tony couldn't stand the thought of facing him right now. Or his mother. Her sympathy was almost as painful as his father's overwhelming interest.

Tony decided to stop at the gym on his way home and swim some laps.

"Tony!" Tim, the gym receptionist, called out to him when he walked in. "Good to see you off those crutches. How's the knee?"

"Fine," Tony said automatically.

"So, can we expect to see you out on the field soon?" he continued.

"I hope so," Tony said quickly. *Everyone asks the same thing,* he thought. *How's the knee, when can we see you back out there? If they only knew how crummy their concern makes me feel!*

"Is it crowded?" Tony asked.

Tim shrugged. "A few of the regulars. Lou's here."

Did he want to see Lou? Tony wondered. And face the same barrage of questions about his knee? Tony nodded briefly at Tim and headed for the locker room. If he changed quickly and went straight to the pool, maybe he could avoid meeting anyone he knew.

In minutes Tony had changed into his swimsuit, taken a quick shower, and headed out to the pool.

The pool was almost empty so late in the day. Tony took a lane to himself. It felt great to swim laps. He felt himself calming down. His breathing was good, his upper body felt strong, even his leg felt good in the water. Tony loved feeling so weightless and so fast.

After twenty-five laps his heart was pounding in his chest, but he didn't stop. *Come on, Tony,* an inner voice cried. *You can do it!* But after one more lap Tony had to stop.

Twenty-six laps, he thought with disgust. Two weeks ago he could have done thirty with hardly any effort. What was happening to him?

As he pulled himself out of the water, Tony felt all the weight in his right leg again. It was like climbing back into pain, and he felt a lump form in his throat. How much longer was this going to last? Plaques and medals of former swimming champions lined the walls of the pool area, and Tony couldn't help reading some of the names as he limped toward the locker room. *Fat chance I'll ever be a champion now*, he thought miserably.

"Tony!" a familiar voice cried as he opened the locker room door straight into a tanned, muscular chest. It was Lou Orton.

"Uh, hi, Lou," Tony said unenthusiastically. He was feeling sorry for himself and was not particularly in the mood for conversation.

Lou followed Tony back inside the locker room. "You're just the guy I was looking for. Tim told me he saw you come in. I don't know how you can stand swimming," he added. "All that chlorine stinging your eyes!"

Tony shrugged. "It's OK," he said.

"So how's the knee? I see you're off your crutches," Lou continued.

"It's fine," Tony said shortly. *Leave me alone*, he thought. *Don't make me go over and over this!*

"It doesn't look as if you're putting all your weight on it," Lou said. He backed off and squinted down at Tony's right leg. "Is it still bugging you?"

"Yeah, a little," Tony admitted. "It's taking longer to heal than I'd hoped." *Talk about the understatement of the year*, he thought unhappily. He should tell Lou the truth. Tony was afraid that at this rate, his knee would *never* get better.

Lou pursed his lips. "Maybe I can help," he said.

"What do you mean?" Tony demanded.

Lou shrugged. "Remember I was telling you about those magic vitamins I've got? A friend of mine's a sports doctor upstate, and he prescribes them for me. They're not cheap, though. And I can only get them for close friends," he added.

Tony looked at Lou suspiciously. "I've been to the doctor twice already and all he's given me is a mild painkiller, sort of like aspirin, and some cortisone pills, which I'm done with," he said.

"Uh, yeah, well, there are different rules in the south of the state. You can only get *these* pills up north," Lou said quickly. He followed Tony to his locker and sat down on the bench while Tony dried off. "It's up to you, but I think these pills could help you out. If you want them," he added. "No one's forcing you."

"I thought you said you guys used them to pump up," Tony said skeptically. "I don't want any bulk on me. I'm a runner, remember?"

Lou nodded. "They do different things depending on how you work out," he explained. "You may bulk up a bit. But if you're not bench pressing, you won't see much change. They'll make you faster, I'll tell you that much. And they'll take care of healing your knee, *fast.*"

If these pills are so great, Tony thought, *why hasn't Dr. Griffin or Suzanne mentioned them?* "I don't know, Lou," he said uncertainly.

"It's up to you," Lou said. "But I'll tell you, I've seen too many guys throw away their careers because of one stupid injury. You get hurt, you slow down, you lose confidence, and somehow, by the end of the season, you're just another good athlete when you could have been a champion."

Lou's words hit Tony hard. Wasn't that exactly what he'd been dreading? Exactly what was beginning to seem inevitable? In another couple of weeks Burr Davidson would forget all about him. In a year somebody else would be the hot new runner and Tony would be nothing, no one.

If Lou was right, if these pills worked fast, he could be competing again instead of sitting on the sidelines. He would be in shape before the All-County meet. And his father would be thrilled.

"Well, if they're really that great . . ." he said slowly.

Lou stood up and thumped him on the shoulder. "Smart guy," he said. "I'll tell you what. Just because I happen to care about what happens to you, I'll get you some right away, for a reduced rate. Ten bucks. What do you say?"

"Thanks, Lou," Tony said gratefully. He followed Lou over to his locker and watched as Lou counted out a handful of pills and put them into a small plastic bag. The pills were light green and a little bigger than daily vitamin pills.

"What are these called?" Tony asked. Before he'd hurt his knee he'd almost never even taken aspirin. Now he felt like a walking medicine cabinet.

Lou shrugged. "I always forget those long medical names." He winked. "Just call them magic vitamins, like the rest of us do. And take them after you eat lunch or dinner," he added. "Otherwise they can bug your stomach."

Tony wadded up the plastic bag and slipped it into his pocket. He took out his wallet and rummaged around for the money. Ten dollars wasn't cheap, that was for sure. But for the first time since the accident Tony felt optimistic. Lou was an athlete; he knew the score. Not like Dr. Griffin and Suzanne, who talked in terms of months and maybes. Lou had promised Tony he'd feel better. And he had promised he'd feel better *fast*.

Tony was in such a good mood at dinner that night, it didn't even upset him when his father asked him, for what must have been the hundredth time since he'd hurt his knee, if he'd heard anything more from Burr Davidson.

When Tony had finished his dinner he excused himself and went into the bathroom on the first floor. He slipped a pale-green tablet out of his pocket and filled a glass with water.

One swallow and it was done. His first magic vitamin. Even as he walked back to the dinner table for dessert, Tony told himself he could feel it working. He was sure that in no time at all, he'd be as good as he'd been before the accident.

"Boy, you're sure in a great mood today," Annie giggled as Tony scooped her up and ran down the hallway Friday afternoon. "Put me down," she cried breathlessly. "Come on, Tony. You're supposed to be taking it easy, remember?"

"Oh yeah," Tony said with a mock growl. "I remember." He set her down and grinned. "I was just trying to sweep you off your feet," he teased her. "It's my way of asking if you'll see a movie with me tonight."

"I'd love to see a movie with you," Annie said happily. "As a matter of fact, I can't think of anything else I'd rather do."

"Can we make it a double date? Roger wants to come, and he's bringing a friend named Sara from Palisades High," Tony asked. "And he'll be bringing Mitch, of course," he added.

"A double date and a half, you mean. Sure, Tony. It sounds like fun."

The two walked down the hall together toward their lockers. "One of the great advantages of being injured," Tony said as he put his arm around her, "is that I don't have to go to practice. I can come and get you early."

"Well, hopefully that won't be the case for much longer. The week after next, or maybe two weeks from now . . ."

Tony laughed. "Didn't I tell you? I'm starting practice again on Monday. Coach and I had a long talk during lunch, and it's all set. Monday at four o'clock, it's *The Return of Tony Esteban*." He laughed again. "Be sure to catch it on a track near you."

"You're going back to practice? Already? But I thought . . ." Annie looked at Tony uncertainly. "I thought Dr. Griffin said you had to wait awhile."

"I've waited," Tony said decisively. "And the knee is healed. I've been timing myself, and yesterday I ran the hundred in near-record time. I'm still a little out of shape, but that's why I've *got* to get right back into practice," he added.

"Listen, I'm thrilled that you're feeling better, but didn't you tell me earlier this week that you didn't think you'd be back at practice for a week or two?"

"I was wrong," Tony replied shortly.

Annie wasn't sure what to think. She was glad Tony was in such a good mood. He'd been so down lately. But this new mood had come on very abruptly, and she wasn't sure she completely trusted it.

"Listen, I'll prove to you how much better I'm feeling. Want me to carry you all the way to cheerleading practice?" Tony asked, grinning down at her.

Annie laughed. "I'll walk, thank you," she told him.

See. I'm an idiot to be so worried about him, Annie scolded herself. It was natural for Tony to have been down after his accident. And now that his knee was healed, it was natural for him to be cheerful and optimistic.

The fact that his knee had gotten better more quickly than any of them expected wasn't a cause for worry, she decided. It was a cause for celebration!

"Todd!" Elizabeth hurried toward Todd in the crowded hallway. It was Friday afternoon, and they still hadn't firmed up their plans for the weekend.

Todd was talking to Aaron Dallas and Winston Egbert. "Can I call you at home, Elizabeth?" Todd asked neutrally.

"I just—" Elizabeth hesitated. "It'll only take a second," she said. She could feel herself blush a little.

"OK, Liz. What's up?" Todd asked once she'd pulled him aside.

Elizabeth looked at Todd with as much flirtatious charm as she could muster. "I was just wondering about tonight, Todd Wilkins. Any chance I could lure you off to some wonderful, private place so we can finally have some time alone together?"

Todd frowned. "You know I've got that meeting tonight, the one about organizing a kids' basketball team."

"I didn't know! You never even mentioned it to me," Elizabeth objected.

"I told you about it—twice. You just weren't listening," Todd said accusingly.

Elizabeth took a deep breath. "Well, tomorrow night, then," she suggested.

Todd shook his head. "Tomorrow night there'll probably be a big party to celebrate the track meet. You know what'll happen. We'll go out with a mob. As usual."

Elizabeth took his hand. "Todd," she said softly.

But Todd wasn't in the mood to talk. "Listen, Aaron and Winston are waiting for me. I'll call you later."

Todd didn't even kiss her goodbye. He just walked off, as if he and Elizabeth were nothing more than buddies. Which, Elizabeth thought unhappily, was feeling more and more like the truth!

Seven

"Hey, look who's here. It's Tony!" yelled Carl Dreyfuss, one of the senior sprinters.

"To-*ny*! To-*ny*!" Roger started chanting.

Soon the whole locker room was cheering. "Good to have you back. We missed you," Carl said, draping one arm around Tony's shoulder as they headed out to the field together.

Tony felt exultant. It was his first day back at practice since his disaster sixteen days before. He could hardly wait to get out on the field.

Tony slid one finger into the small inner pocket of the training shorts he was wearing. Sure enough, that day's magic vitamin was there. After not even a week of taking the pills, Tony was already convinced that they were not only magical but miraculous. The pain in his knee had almost completely vanished. He felt more alive, full of energy and strength. In fact, he'd never felt as good about his physical condition as he did right then. He was sure he could get out there on the field and beat anyone.

Tony's times during this first practice weren't the greatest they'd ever been, and Roger beat him twice in sprints. But still, Tony felt euphoric. When Coach Featherston snapped a towel at him and said, in his usual grudging fashion, "Not bad for the first day back, Esteban," he felt like giving the man a hug.

"Just give me a bit more time. I'll whip you," he called out to Roger in the shower room.

"Hey, take it easy," Roger said mildly. "I'm on the same team as you, remember?"

But Tony didn't hear him. He was doing some fast arithmetic in his head as he showered. That night, after dinner, he would take another magic vitamin. That would leave him with only four. It was clear to Tony that he shouldn't stop taking them now, not when they were doing him so much good.

I'd better stop off at the gym tonight or tomorrow night to see Lou, he told himself. *I don't want to run out of these things now. Especially not when we've got a meet this Saturday against San Pedro High. Everyone will be out there, expecting great things from me. Including Dad.*

Tony knew that when he saw Lou and told him how great the pills were Lou would say, "I told you so." Tony smiled ruefully, turned

73

off the shower, and reached for his towel. But so what? Lou had been right, hadn't he?

If I'd waited and taken Dr. Griffin's advice, I'd probably still be sitting on the bench, Tony reminded himself. As far as he was concerned, Lou had every reason to be smug about those pills of his.

It wasn't until he got back to his locker and started to dress that a little voice in the back of his head reminded Tony that he didn't really know what was in the pills.

I shouldn't just go and buy more of them, he thought uneasily as he slipped his polo shirt over his head. *Not without asking Lou more about them. Not without finding out what these magic vitamins really are.*

Tim looked up when Tony breezed through the door of the gym Monday evening.

"You're looking a lot better," he said cheerfully.

Tony nodded. "Yeah, I feel great. My knee hardly hurts anymore," he said.

"That's great. That means I can put my bets on you for the All-County," Tim continued with a grin.

"Is Lou here?" Tony asked, glancing at his watch. His parents liked him to be on time for dinner. His only reason for stopping by the gym was to find Lou and get a fresh supply of pills.

"Yeah, he's here," Tim said. He turned away to answer a phone call.

Tony hurried back to the men's locker room, but there was no sign of Lou. "He's in the weight room," Randy told him.

Tony nodded and headed back to the smaller of the two weight rooms, the one he knew Lou favored. Sure enough, he was there, hard at work at the bench press. He sat up when he saw Tony.

"Hey, how's it going? Is your knee any better?" he asked. Tony thought he sounded really concerned, as though it mattered to him whether or not Tony healed quickly. *I can't believe I ever mistrusted him,* Tony thought.

"Yeah, it's a lot better. I can't believe how great those pills are," Tony said effusively.

Lou glanced quickly at the door of the weight room. "Yeah, they really are," he said. "But let's keep it under wraps, OK? I don't want any of the other guys bugging me for them. Just close friends. If the word gets out, I'll never be able to supply enough of them."

Tony was quiet for a minute. "Yeah, well, that's what I wanted to talk to you about. I'm going to need more of them. We've got a lot of big meets coming up, and my knee still has a way to go."

Lou shrugged. "Fine. I can get you a month's supply. That's about as many as I can get hold of at any one time. You got a hundred dollars?"

"A hundred—" Tony stared at him. "But . . ."

"Ten dollars was a special deal. I told you. I gave you a cut for the first week. But the guy I'm getting them from raised his prices." Lou shrugged again. "It's up to you. You don't have to buy them from me if you don't want to. It's a free country."

Tony felt his face flush. Several images raced through his head. He saw Burr Davidson and the other talent scouts, watching him at the All-County. He saw an Olympic medal. Last, he imagined the look of joy and pride on his father's face if he could pull it off, if he could really make it as a professional track star. "No, I want to!" Tony cried. He realized he sounded desperate. "I'll get the money," he said more calmly. "Just tell me when you can get me the pills."

Lou thought. "Let's see. Today's Monday. I don't go up to see that friend of mine until the weekend. Let's say I can have them early next week."

Tony bit his lip. He had only four left. What was he supposed to do once they ran out?

"Sorry," Lou said with another shrug. "It's the best I can do."

Tony nodded. "OK," he said quickly. "See you next week, then."

"Yeah." Lou nodded. "Don't forget the money. A hundred dollars, cash. No money, no pills." He winked at Tony. "Just ask Randy if you don't believe me. I'm terrible when guys can't pay."

Tony swallowed. He was going to have to dip into the money he'd been saving to put air conditioning in his Mazda. And he'd have to scrap his plans to take Annie somewhere on the weekend.

Even so, he was lucky. At least he *had* the money. He couldn't imagine how he'd feel if he didn't.

Tony was all the way out in the parking lot when he realized he hadn't remembered to ask Lou what was really in the pills. For a brief moment Tony considered going back to find him. But it was already twenty minutes to seven, and he didn't want to be any later to dinner than he already was.

He'd ask Lou some other time. Anyway, Lou hadn't seemed as friendly this time as he had been before. Tony had a feeling that when it came to business, Lou was even tougher than he was on the wrestling mat.

"What's the matter with you?" Jessica asked her twin.

It was Tuesday afternoon, and Jessica had gotten home early from cheerleading practice to find Elizabeth sitting in the living room, staring into space.

"This isn't like you," Jessica commented. "Usually you're busy writing something for the newspaper or doing something else equally constructive with your spare time." She sat down on the couch and inspected her sister intently. "I don't see what you can possibly be upset about. You don't have to spend your Tuesday evening addressing a local junior high as Miss Teen Sweet Valley."

Elizabeth sighed. "The truth is, I don't have *anything* to do tonight. I was supposed to go over to Todd's house to study. Only guess what? He canceled on me."

"So?" Jessica said with an unsympathetic shrug. "Big deal. Can't you study here?"

"You don't understand. Todd's been . . . oh, I don't know, *different*," Elizabeth said. Her voice sounded like it was close to breaking. "I think he's really upset with me, only he won't talk about it. Remember I told you that he thought we needed more private time together, more time to be just a twosome? Well, I didn't take him seriously enough. And now he doesn't seem to *want* to be alone with me. Now he only wants to do things in big groups. I was the one who had the idea to study alone together tonight, and he just called and told me he isn't feeling very well."

Jessica frowned. "Hmm. Sounds like he's paying you back, giving you a taste of your own medicine."

"Todd wouldn't do that," Elizabeth protested. "Would he?" Elizabeth looked helplessly at her twin.

"Why not?" Jessica said. "Listen, why don't you plan a really romantic evening with him?

It sounds to me as if all you two need is one really fantastic night together to get the chemistry back. Why don't you kidnap him and take him up to Miller's Point?" she suggested with a giggle.

"Kidnap him . . ." Elizabeth mused. "You know, you're pretty smart for a beauty pageant winner. You may have hit on something," she cried.

Jessica was right. She and Todd needed more than time alone together; they needed some thrilling romance! Kidnapping Todd might just be the answer. She'd been too insensitive to hear him when he had been pleading with her for some time alone. Now she was going to have to take extreme measures to show him she'd gotten his message loud and clear.

Tony felt better and better over the course of the next several days. Friday, at lunchtime, he took the last of the pills Lou had given him. He wondered uneasily what it would be like for the next few days without the magic vitamins. He still couldn't believe what a difference Lou's pills were making.

The pain was now completely gone from his injured knee. Even when he ran at top speed he didn't feel a single twinge. And not only was he running as fast as he had before the injury, but during the last practice he'd actually beaten his own best time in the 220.

But it wasn't just that he was running faster. Tony felt strong, clearheaded, on top of the world. He actually felt as if he was breathing more efficiently! He didn't seem to need as much sleep, and he seemed to be concentrating better in his classes.

The only thing that didn't feel better was his relationship with Annie. He had no idea why, but over the past few days he'd felt himself withdrawing from her. All he wanted to think about was running, and Annie got in the way of that.

They'd made plans to go out on the weekend, but Tony wasn't as enthusiastic as he had been earlier in the week. Roger asked him about it after practice on Friday.

"You and Annie going out tonight?"

Tony shook his head. "Tomorrow, I think. I haven't really figured out what we're going to do."

"Annie's a nice girl. And she really seems to like you," Roger commented. "You're lucky."

Tony worked some deep-heat rub into his leg. "I don't know," he said with a sigh. "She's a little . . . I'm not even sure I know the right word for it. She *worries* about me. She asks me five times a day how my knee is doing. It's been bugging me a little."

Roger looked surprised. "I wouldn't mind having a girl like Annie worry about *me*."

Tony shrugged. "It's just an important time for me right now. All I can think about is the

80

All-County meet. I'm so psyched up about running against San Pedro High tomorrow, I can't even think about Annie. You know what I mean?"

"Not really." Roger grinned. "But maybe that's why I'm not slated for the Olympics and you are. I don't have that killer instinct." He raised his eyebrows. "I guess it's kind of different now, huh? Now that you've got Burr Davidson and these other big scouts watching you? Running's not just for fun anymore. The stakes are a lot higher."

"Yeah," Tony agreed. "You're right, Roger. My dad's been talking to me a lot about my attitude. He keeps saying that it isn't only muscle or talent that makes an athlete. It's your mental state. You've got to want to kill the competition."

Roger looked surprised. "Your dad said that?"

Tony nodded. "He's also not so sure that getting close to Annie is the best thing for me right now," he confided.

"Maybe I shouldn't say anything, but your dad may not be right on this one," Roger said.

"He's *always* right when it comes to me!" Tony said passionately. Roger hadn't known his own father. He didn't know how crucial a father's advice and support could be.

Tony was about to say something more when two seniors from the team walked into the locker room and opened lockers right next to Tony and Roger.

"I couldn't believe it either," Dan Conway said.

Nick Hudson shook his head. "I just can't believe someone like Don would take steroids," he said incredulously.

"I know. But my brother's best friends with his roommate at Sweet Valley College and he told my brother the whole story. Apparently Don got really obsessive about winning the college title in men's butterfly, and someone he knew got him started on steroids. The coaches found out and he was cut from the team. It stinks. Don was a champion swimmer."

Roger and Tony looked at each other. They didn't mean to listen to the boys' conversation, but it was hard not to.

Nick opened his locker and took out a towel. "I didn't know swimmers took steroids. I thought they were just for weightlifters."

"I don't know all that much about them, but supposedly a lot of guys take them to improve their speed. My brother told me they make your blood process oxygen more efficiently."

Tony looked down uneasily at the floor. Steroids. He'd heard about them, sure. No one who was serious about sports hadn't. But what were they, exactly? He didn't know much more about them than Nick or Dan did. He knew they were illegal, and he had a vague sense that they might be dangerous, though he wasn't completely sure why.

A terrible thought suddenly occurred to him,

82

but he tried to block it out. What was it Lou had said about Randy? That he'd put on twenty pounds of muscle since he'd started taking his magic vitamins?

Lou's pills couldn't be steroids, could they?

Tony took a deep breath. He wished Dan and Nick hadn't come in when they had, that he hadn't overheard their conversation, because now he knew he was going to have to talk to Lou. Before he took another one of those pills, he had to find out what they really were.

Eight

"You see?" Elizabeth complained to Enid on Saturday night. "This is the way all my dates with Todd have been for the past couple of weeks! We're always surrounded by people. I can't remember the last time we had a romantic evening, just the two of us."

Right then Elizabeth was sitting so far away from Todd, she didn't have to lower her voice to confide in her best friend. They were at the Dairi Burger as part of a spontaneous victory party for the track team, which had demolished San Pedro High that afternoon. A big group had gathered at several of the back tables, including Roger, Tony, Annie, Elizabeth, Todd, Enid, John Pfeifer, Winston Egbert, and Mitch Ferguson, who was glued to Tony's side, listening attentively to everything he said.

"Aren't you having a good time?" Enid asked.

"Of course I am," Elizabeth said slowly. "It's just . . ."

Just that Todd was right, and I didn't listen to him when it mattered, she thought unhappily. That afternoon, sitting with him at the track meet, she'd suggested they drive to the canyon that night and look at the stars. Just as the words were out of her mouth, Winston had run up to tell them that if Sweet Valley won, the whole crowd was going to meet at the Dairi Burger. "Sounds great," Todd had said without even a glance at Elizabeth for confirmation.

So much for a chance to be alone.

"Listen, I'm going to need your help," Elizabeth told Enid. "I don't think telling Todd how much I miss being alone with him is working. I'm going to have to *show* him." She pulled her friend closer to her and whispered her plan.

"This is nuts," Enid said after a moment. "We can't talk here. I know—come with me to the girls' bathroom."

It took a minute or two to wriggle out from behind the crowded table, but they managed it. They didn't manage to get out alone, though. "Let me come with you guys," Annie Whitman said, with an anxious glance back at Tony.

"Hey, *you* must be having fun tonight," Elizabeth said to Annie when they'd closed the bathroom door behind them.

Annie fussed with a small makeup bag she'd taken out of her purse. "Yeah," she said uncertainly. "Listen, you guys, have you noticed anything different about Tony lately?"

Elizabeth and Enid glanced at each other. "What do you mean?" Enid asked.

"Doesn't he seem . . . I can't really describe it very well . . . a little more competitive than he used to be? You know, the way he's going on and on about the guys he faced off against today in the meet?"

"Maybe it's just because he's in the middle of the track season," Enid suggested.

"And being injured probably made a difference in his attitude. Tony may feel he has to work extra hard to win back the place he had before he fell," Elizabeth added.

"I've thought of both those things," Annie conceded. "But—"

"Listen, Todd sometimes gets really worked up in the middle of basketball season," Elizabeth said reassuringly.

Annie shook her head. "I just have this weird feeling lately that Tony's changed. He's much more *intense*, more nervous than he used to be. He never jokes about the coach, or practice, or about anything sports-related anymore. It's like he's obsessed."

"God, sometimes I hate sports," Enid said sympathetically. "He probably needs you more than ever, Annie."

"I don't think so." Annie's green eyes were filled with unhappiness. "Lately he's been impatient with me. To tell you the truth, I don't really know what's going to happen between us. I'm not sure Tony and I are that well-suited for each other after all."

Elizabeth felt bad. Only a few weeks before, Annie had been so excited about Tony. "Annie, are you sure it's not just the pressure of an important season getting to him? You're sure things won't be better once Tony's past the All-County meet?"

"That's still a month away," Annie said. "And the way things are going between us right now, I'd be surprised if we make it that long." She shrugged. "I like Tony a lot. I guess all I can do is wait it out for a while and see what happens."

It saddened Elizabeth to think that a relationship that had seemed so promising was falling apart so quickly. But Annie struck her as pretty astute. If she claimed Tony was unhappy with the relationship, she was probably right.

Tony didn't want the party at the Dairi Burger to end. He was having a great time going over and over the fine points of his races earlier that day.

Mitch was openly interested. "Tell me again how you knew what strategy that guy from the other school would use," he demanded.

Tony leaned back in his seat. "If you really want me to," he said, secretly glad to relive the scene. "See, I've known Dennis Forbes for a while. He always does the same thing when he sprints. He uses up almost all his energy in the first forty or fifty yards, giving him an edge which scares off a lot of other runners. All I did today was let him take the lead, then gained on him at the first turn of the 220." He grinned. "I showed him, too!"

Roger shifted a little in his seat. "Yeah, you were great," he said. His voice sounded a little less enthusiastic than it had earlier, but Tony hadn't noticed.

"That's cool." Mitch's eyes were shining. "Maybe this running stuff isn't so bad after all."

"It's the best thing on earth," Tony said vehemently. He could still remember the rush he'd felt as he crouched down to run. It had been an absolutely perfect day, from beginning to end. Only one thing marred it for Tony, and that was the realization that he'd taken the last of his magic vitamins the day before.

The thought of missing a few days made Tony feel uncomfortable. True, he couldn't be absolutely certain that the pills were what was making him feel so good. But it sure looked that way. His times that day had been better than they'd ever been. *If only Burr Davidson had been there*, Tony thought for the thousandth time since the meet. But that was OK. There was always next time.

"Sorry about you and Clements," Tony said

to Roger. Sam Clements had beaten Roger in his second race.

"Yeah," Roger said, shrugging. "It happens. I was having an off day, I guess."

"I watched you pretty closely. You're dragging your right heel. I've got some exercises you should try," Tony said.

Roger didn't say anything, and his silence made Tony feel free to continue his critique. "Also, when you crouch with your palms down the way you do, you lose a half-second off your start," Tony continued.

"Wow," Mitch said admiringly. "You know an awful lot about running, Tony!"

"Yeah, he sure does," Roger said with just a hint of sarcasm.

Tony was just about to give Roger some more pointers when Annie got up from the table. "Listen, Tony, I promised my mom I'd be back by midnight."

Tony stared at her. For a split second he didn't understand what she was getting at. Then he remembered. She'd come with him, and he was supposed to take her home. *What a pain*, he thought as he got reluctantly to his feet. He would much rather talk about the meet with Roger than end the evening early to take Annie home.

"Sorry about that," she said when they were out in the parking lot.

"Yeah, well, you couldn't help it." Tony was rapidly forgetting his annoyance with Annie.

He was beginning to worry again about how he was going to feel the next day without Lou's pills. Just the thought of another day without the magic vitamins seemed to make his injured knee feel sensitive. It actually throbbed a little as he climbed into his Mazda.

"Tony, are you OK?" Annie asked suddenly. "You look upset."

"I'm fine," he said, more quickly than he'd intended. He didn't want Annie worrying about him. Over the last day or two he'd managed to ignore the disturbing idea that he might be taking steroids without knowing it. Annie's concern only reminded him that maybe he really did have something to worry about.

They drove to Annie's apartment complex in silence. Tony parked his car in front and looked up automatically at the windows he knew were hers. The lights were on. Her mother was waiting up for her.

Suddenly, a wave of regret washed over him for the way he'd been behaving. He liked Annie. She didn't have anything to do with Lou Orton, the magic vitamins, or his father's pressure. She liked him for who he was, not what he was—a good runner hoping to be the best. So why was he brushing her off like this?

"Annie, do me a favor," he said, trying to keep his voice even. "Be patient with me, OK? I know I've been obsessed with my running lately. It's just that I've got a lot of pressure on me right now."

Annie fiddled with the door handle. "I can't tell if you want to be with me anymore," she said sadly.

"I've been acting like an idiot. I like you, Annie. I really do." Tony looked anxiously at her. Suddenly it seemed urgent that she understand, that she stick by him.

"Look, I like you, too, Tony. But I'm pretty confused. For the past several days . . ." Her voice trailed off uncertainly. "I appreciate how hard it must be for you, getting hurt right at the beginning of the season. But it seems as if you're losing perspective."

Tony bit his lip. "Don't bail out on me, Annie," he said again. He took her hand in his. "I've got so much riding on this season. Once it's over I could have a scholarship to any state school I want. I might even have a shot at the Olympics. Four more weeks and my life will go back to normal. I promise."

Annie looked at him uncertainly. "OK," she said at last. "I'll hang in there. But Tony, I'm not sure you can divide your life up like that. I'm not sure you can switch on one kind of behavior during track season and expect to switch it off when the season's over."

Tony didn't answer. *Annie doesn't even know the worst of it*, he thought uneasily. She was upset with him because he'd been more intense, more aggressive. Imagine how she'd feel if she knew he'd been taking pills to make his speed better. And that he didn't know what was in those pills.

Still, his spirits lifted a little as he drove home. He was glad he'd talked to Annie. He'd realized again that night that he really did care about her.

It wasn't until he was almost home that Tony realized he'd gone against his father's wishes. He'd taken steps to get closer to Annie, instead of letting things trail off.

Maybe his father *wasn't* right when it came to Annie, Tony thought. It wasn't an easy idea to accept. His dad was *always* right, about everything. He was the one who had said again and again that winning was the most important thing in life. Was it possible he was wrong about that, too?

Nine

Tony headed over to the gym right after break-fast on Sunday morning. His knee was both-ering him, and he was certain he wasn't just imagining things. For the first time in a while, the thought of running wasn't appealing.

Lou wasn't in the weight room or the locker room, and Tony started to get anxious. "You haven't seen him at all?" he asked Tim.

"Nope. Not yet," Tim said.

Tony paced up and down the lobby. He had a headache, and he felt irritable. After about fifteen minutes, he decided to leave. "Tell Lou I was looking for him," he said abruptly as he headed out to the parking lot.

When he got outside, he saw Lou's blue Mustang pull up. Lou got out, wearing a pair of mirrored sunglasses. "Hi, Tony. What's up?" he said.

"I wanted to know if you got the pills," Tony said. He knew he sounded too urgent, and it didn't make him feel better when Lou laughed.

"Easy, guy." Lou took his sunglasses off and gave Tony a studied grin. "I guess they're working, huh?"

Tony didn't answer. "You haven't answered my question," he said in a low voice. "Did you get any more?"

"Not yet, pal. I told you, they'll be here in a couple of days. Just relax." Lou's expression looked a little less friendly than it had a moment earlier, and Tony felt a stab of uneasiness.

"You never told me what's in those things," Tony said quickly.

Lou's expression suddenly turned cold. "Listen, you want to be a customer, right? Because I've got two rules for customers. The first is, they pay cash. The second is, they don't ask me any questions. Got it?"

Tony's mouth was dry. It was all too clear. He knew that from this point on he should have absolutely nothing to do with Lou. If there wasn't something dangerous or illegal about those pills, Lou would have told him straight out what was in them.

And then Tony thought of his father and the Olympics and the scholarships, and he knew what he was going to do: get a fresh supply of pills. He needed them, at least until the All-County meet. Once he'd done well in that meet, he vowed he'd never go near Lou and his pills again.

Lou looked at him closely. "You understand the ground rules?" he asked.

Tony nodded. "Yeah," he said. One short, horrible syllable.

"OK. Meet me Tuesday afternoon, right here. Bring the hundred bucks, and I'll give you your pills. And quit following me around. It doesn't look right." Lou stepped around Tony and strolled toward the gym.

Tony felt sick to his stomach. What kind of mess had he gotten himself into?

It isn't too late, a voice inside him protested. *Just walk away from this place and don't come back.*

Coach Featherston was in a terrible mood on Monday. Instead of praising the track team for their win against San Pedro over the weekend, he assembled the team and bawled them out. "You guys aren't serious athletes, not one of you. Half of you are late to practice and the other half aren't trying. How are you going to win the All-County meet if you don't get your act together?"

It was a pretty typical speech for Coach Featherston, and ordinarily it wouldn't have bothered Tony. But that afternoon the coach's words got under his skin. He hadn't taken one of Lou's pills since Friday, and he was dreading the moment when he had to get out on the field and run.

He heard the coach's message, loud and clear. *If you are a serious athlete, you make sacrifices. You put your heart and soul into your sport. You don't treat it like just another hobby.*

"OK! Now I want to see you out on the field, and I want to see your best stuff," the coach bellowed. He blew his whistle to signal that the lecture was over.

"Nice speech, huh?" Roger said, loping beside Tony out to the track.

Tony shrugged. "He's got a point. We *do* look kind of sloppy."

Roger raised his eyebrows. "I've never once heard you agree with Coach Featherston! Don't tell me he's been brainwashing you in your sleep?"

"Aw, get out of here," Tony said, giving Roger a playful slug on the shoulder as they ran. He didn't mean to hit him hard, but the surprised look on Roger's face told Tony he had.

Tony didn't have time to apologize. The coach blew his whistle again and organized pairs for timed sprints. "Roger, Tony, why don't you start off," he barked.

The two boys took their positions at the starting line. The rest of the team gathered to watch. One short blow of the coach's whistle and they were off.

Tony felt his heart sink with the first two

strides. His knee didn't feel right and his leg was dragging a little. *Get it together, Esteban,* he commanded himself. Roger pulled out in front of him and Tony began to gasp. He couldn't let Roger beat him. He couldn't. He just—

Almost unconsciously, Tony's arm flew out and hit Roger as the two boys rounded the only curve of the sprint. Roger stumbled, caught himself, and began to run again. But that instant was all Tony needed to take the lead. He pulled ahead and crossed the finish line a split second before Roger.

"What did you do out there?" Roger gasped as the two boys bent over, trying to catch their breath. "You shoved me! What's wrong with you, anyway?"

Tony couldn't believe it had happened. It was like something in a nightmare. "I didn't do anything," he said defensively. And then he added, "Sorry. It was an accident."

Coach Featherston came over with his stopwatch and glared at them both. Apparently he hadn't seen Tony's shove. "Pretty poor showing for my two top sprinters," he said. He read them their times, and Tony felt ill. He may have beaten Roger, but his time was three seconds slower than it had been the week before.

"I don't know what's going on with you lately," Roger snapped at him later in the locker room. "But you'd better chill out, Esteban.

Winning may be important, but I'm on *your* team, remember?"

Tony nodded absently and headed for the showers. He soaped up and tried not to think about anything. Thinking was too hard these days. When had everything become so complicated?

Just that morning at breakfast his father had given him a present: a gift certificate to use at the best sporting-goods store in Sweet Valley. "I want you to know how proud I am of you, son," Mr. Esteban had said. Tony had looked uneasily at the certificate and avoided his father's eyes. His father's pride in him didn't feel good anymore. It felt like a burden.

The minute the coach read him his abysmal time, Tony silently confirmed his decision to meet Lou at the gym the next afternoon.

He didn't care what was in those pills. The All-County meet was three weeks from Saturday, and Tony had to give it everything. Once the meet was over and he had Burr Davidson's support for scholarships and the Olympic trials, he'd never touch another pill, not as long as he lived.

"Tell me again what you're saying," Winston Egbert said to Todd. "You want to *kidnap* your own girlfriend?" It was Tuesday, and the two boys were eating lunch together. Todd had explained to Winston that Elizabeth was spending her lunch hour in the *Oracle* office trying to meet a deadline.

"It's the only way," Todd said. "Listen, Winston. You know how crazy I am about Liz. But she's so committed to helping other people, she barely has any time left for herself or for me! John Pfeifer's asked her to help him cover the track season, so she's got yet *another* big commitment." Todd shook his head. "Every time we try to do something, just the two of us, we end up in the middle of a mob scene. Look at last Saturday night, for example."

"I usually don't like to be considered just one of the mob," Winston wisecracked. "But I see your point. You want to prove to Liz that you adore her. So, how are you going to kidnap her?"

"Well, that's where you come in. I haven't got all the details ironed out yet. In fact, I haven't really got a plan at all. I just know I want to find some really romantic spot and instead of telling her about it, I want you to kidnap her. You know, a blindfold, the whole works. And when the blindfold is removed, I'll be waiting for her!"

"OK, Wilkins," Winston said. "You've got yourself a partner in crime. Just tell me when and where, and I promise to produce one blind-folded blond Wakefield twin for a little lesson in romance!"

* * *

On Thursday, Elizabeth and Enid were deep in conversation at lunchtime when Annie Whitman stopped next to them holding her tray. "My usual lunch crowd abandoned me," she said with a smile. "Any room here for an interloper?"

"Pull up a chair," Enid said warmly.

"How are things with Tony?" Elizabeth asked her. "Any better?"

Annie looked a little embarrassed. "I'm not completely sure. We've got a date for this weekend, and he's called me a few times this week. But he just doesn't seem like himself. He's still really tense."

Elizabeth sighed. "There must be some kind of terrible anti-romance virus going around. And I thought Todd and I were the only ones afflicted."

Enid giggled. "How is the kidnapping scheme going? You haven't mentioned it."

"Well, actually, I could use a little bit of help," Elizabeth admitted. "I know exactly what I want to do. I want to find some incredible, romantic, out-of-the-way restaurant and make a reservation for dinner. And then I need somebody, or somebodies, to kidnap Todd and bring him to me at the restaurant."

"That sounds like a fantastic idea!" Annie's eyes sparkled. "I'd be happy to help kidnap Todd. In fact, I've got a special guidebook you can use to find a really neat place. It's called *Weekend Getaways*."

"I'd love to borrow it," Elizabeth said.

Annie frowned. "I wonder . . . oh yeah. I remember what I did with it. I loaned it to Tony." She sighed. "Given the current circumstances, I don't think he'll be studying it in his spare time. Lately, unless it involves a track and a stopwatch, it doesn't appeal to him."

"Well, if you can get the book back from Tony, let me know," Elizabeth said.

"It's in his locker," she said. "Come on, let's get it now." She grinned. "If I can't have any romance in my own life, at least I can help you put some back in yours!"

"You're sure you want to go into his locker?" Elizabeth asked. "I can wait, Annie."

"No, come on. I need to get my math book, too. Tony has my combination and I have his," Annie insisted.

A few minutes later Annie, Elizabeth, and Enid had returned their trays and were headed down the hall to the lockers.

"Let's see. . . ." Annie tried three numbers and the locker popped open. "Tony's so messy," she said with a fond smile as she looked at the jumbled contents of his locker. She moved his jacket aside. "Here's my math book," she said. "Now, the guidebook must be somewhere down here. . . ."

"I wouldn't want anyone looking through *my* locker. It's a lot messier than this," Enid said with a laugh.

Just then Annie pulled out a bottle of pills.

A frown crossed her face. "I wonder what these are," she said, looking at them thoughtfully.

"They're probably the pills the doctor gave Tony for his leg," Elizabeth suggested.

Annie shook her head. "I don't think so. He finished those a while ago."

Elizabeth looked uncomfortable. "Maybe we should just get the book and go," she said quickly.

Annie nodded absently. "Yeah, you're right." *What kind of medicine could Tony possibly be taking at this point?* she thought. She was sure Dr. Griffin's prescription had run out after one week. But this bottle had enough pills in it to last about a month.

Annie bent over and rummaged for the guidebook. It took her a minute to find it, enough time for her to pry the lid off the bottle and sneak out a single pill. Tony would never miss it. And in the meantime Annie intended to find out exactly what they were.

Ten

"OK, guys," Elizabeth said to Enid and Annie on Friday at lunchtime. "I've read Annie's guidebook, and I've found the perfect place to steal Todd away to. It's called Castillo San Angelo. It's a beautiful old house that was built by an eccentric Spaniard at the turn of the century. It's an hour away from here, and it's got a restaurant and beautiful gardens. It sounds absolutely perfect." Her eyes shone. "I've already made reservations. Dinner for two, a week from tomorrow night. Do you guys think you can get Todd there somehow?"

Enid giggled. "Sure! Maybe we'll pretend we're taking him on a scavenger hunt." She winked at Annie. "Don't worry, Liz. We'll deliver him to this castillo of yours. All you have to do is give us directions."

Winston approached with his lunch tray and

suddenly stopped short. "Girls!" he said. "Any room for a lonely male here, or do I have to eat my lunch all alone, without your charming conversation?"

"Sit down," Enid said dryly. "But we can't promise much in the way of charm."

A copy of the page advertising Castillo San Angelo lay on the table and Winston's eye happened to fall on it as he was setting down his tray. "Nice," he said. "Don't tell me the Wakefields are buying a little place in the country."

Elizabeth laughed. "Don't I wish," she said casually. She didn't want Winston finding out too much about Castillo San Angelo. He and Todd were good friends, and he might blow her secret.

But there was no way to keep Winston from asking questions. "A real castle, right here in southern California. I thought you had to go to Europe for that sort of thing," he said.

Elizabeth sighed. Well, as long as Winston didn't know about her scheme, what harm could it do if he discovered the particulars of Castillo San Angelo? Elizabeth described it to him, leaving out the information about the restaurant. "Sounds romantic," Winston said. "Mind if I borrow this paper, Liz? My—uh, my mother's looking for a special place to take my dad on his birthday."

"I guess it's OK," Elizabeth said slowly. She knew that if she acted too secretive about it,

Winston, or worse, Todd, might guess that she was up to something!

Annie woke up late on Sunday morning. At first she couldn't remember what had been making her feel so anxious about today, and then it all came flooding back to her. She was meeting her cousin Beth for lunch, and Beth was going to tell her what she'd found about the pill Annie had sneaked out of Tony's locker.

For the past several days, Annie had felt as if she'd been living a lie. Taking one of Tony's pills without his knowledge was a terrible thing to do. It was like stealing; in a way, it was worse than stealing. Tony had trusted her to use his locker, and she'd tampered with his private property. And then she'd taken the pill to her cousin, who was a graduate student in biochemistry at the state university.

Annie felt sick and ashamed every time she thought about what she'd done. But the minute she'd seen those pills in Tony's locker she'd realized how worried about him she'd been. Initially Annie had assumed that any serious athlete would be depressed after injuring himself at the start of an important season. She'd expected that it might take a while before Tony acted like his old self again.

But now Annie was certain Tony wasn't just moody. Something else was going on. One minute he'd be tense and irritable, and the next minute he'd seem euphoric. He even looked a little different. He seemed slightly more muscular than when they'd first started dating. Sometimes when he hugged her it felt as if he was crushing her.

Worst of all, though, was Tony's new attitude about his sport. One of the reasons Annie had been attracted to Tony in the first place was because of his well-roundedness. Yes, he was an incredible athlete, but he had never acted as if the world would end if he lost a meet. Now the slightest setback seemed to throw him completely. One bad practice and he was on edge for days.

Annie wasn't the only one who'd noticed the change in Tony. The night before, a group including Mitch, Roger, Annie, Tony, Winston, and Carl Dreyfuss had gone bowling. Carl, Tony, and Annie made up one team. Roger, Mitch, and Winston made up another.

From the way Tony had acted, Annie recalled, anyone would have thought they were competing in the Olympics, not just against a bunch of friends. At one point Tony had actually yelled at Annie because she had thrown a few gutter balls. Carl had been embarrassed and had, somewhat jokingly, reminded Tony they were only playing a game.

Annie had been annoyed by Tony's behavior. But at least she was old enough to defend herself. What happened with Mitch had been really painful to watch.

Mitch had changed since that afternoon a few weeks back when they had played miniature golf together. He still wore his obscure rock-group T-shirts, but his expression wasn't as sullen or as mean. At the bowling alley, he had wanted to be on Tony's team. When he wound up on Roger's team, he had looked really disappointed.

"Come on, Mitch! You're up!" Roger had called toward the end of the evening when the two teams were just about tied.

"I hope he throws a gutter ball," Tony had grumbled, loud enough so that Mitch could hear.

Mitch had looked confused, but Winston and Roger had urged him on. Annie wasn't sure exactly what had happened next. Maybe Mitch *had* stepped over the line a little. But if he had, she was sure he hadn't meant to. He was just a kid, and it was just a game among friends! But Tony had gone crazy. He yelled that Mitch had cheated, that they couldn't count his strike. Roger and Winston had defended Mitch, but after Tony's outburst no one felt like finishing the game. No one but Tony, of course, who wanted nothing more than to win.

Annie had tried to comfort Mitch. "I didn't cheat, I didn't," he had repeated unhappily. He had stared at Tony with an expression of such confusion that Annie thought her heart would break.

"I know. Don't worry about it," she had said awkwardly.

Annie and Tony had argued about the episode all the way home. And when she'd gotten into bed she'd asked herself, not for the first time, why she was still seeing Tony. *This recent behavior just isn't normal,* she had told herself stubbornly. *The real Tony Esteban would never have yelled at a kid about something so stupid as stepping over a line.*

But where *was* the real Tony? What had happened to him?

Annie had arranged to meet her cousin at the Box Tree Café in downtown Sweet Valley. She was so eager to hear what Beth would have to tell her that she was fifteen minutes early.

Beth arrived exactly on time. Annie noted that at twenty-four Beth looked almost the same as she had when she was fifteen and had won every science prize at Sweet Valley High. She was tall; her light brown hair, which she wore long, and her horn-rimmed glasses made her look like a college professor. As a graduate student, she had access to a fully-equipped lab.

"Hi, Annie. Did you order yet?" Beth asked as she sat down at the table.

Annie shook her head. She was too nervous to think about food. But Beth always had an appetite. Annie waited tensely while her cousin scrutinized the menu and finally ordered.

"OK," Beth said. She pushed her glasses up on her nose and studied her cousin with interest. "I'm glad you came to me, Annie, but I'm not really sure what kind of advice to give you about your friend. Do you know him very well?"

"We've been going out for a while. I like him a lot. At least, I used to like him a lot. But he's been acting strange lately," Annie said. She leaned closer to her cousin. "Tell me what you found out, Beth."

"Have you ever heard of steroids?" Beth asked.

"Steroids?" Annie repeated. "I think so. A runner in the last Olympics was caught taking them. His gold medal was taken away, and didn't he get kicked off the national team?"

"That's right," Beth said. "To make all this simple, there are two classes of steroid drugs. The first class, sometimes prescribed by doctors, is used to reduce inflammation to tissue. You've heard of cortisone. That's a steroid hormone. But it's the second class that makes the news all the time. This second kind of steroid is more or less a form of male hormone. Guys tend to deal it in locker rooms. It doesn't really have any medicinal value, though some athletes *mistakenly* believe it can help heal injuries." She shook her head. "That kind of steroid is illegal, and, improperly used, can be very dangerous."

"And that's what Tony's been taking? Steroids?" Annie asked quietly.

"The pill you gave me belongs to that second class, yes. If he's been taking them for a while, you may be right when you say his personality has changed. No one is completely sure of the behavioral changes associated with steroid use. But most users report that they become more aggressive, more competitive. They may also bulk up a little. Some complain of headaches and irritability."

"That sure sounds like Tony," Annie said slowly. "But why do people take steroids if they're illegal and if all they do is make you more aggressive and give you headaches?"

Beth shrugged. "The claim is that they produce a greater number of oxygen-carrying cells in the blood. In sports talk, that means you can run faster, swim faster, whatever. You've got more strength, more stamina, more competitive urge. I'm not sure if it's true, or if the results are largely psychological. But the sad truth is, guys can really mess themselves up with steroids. In the wrong dosage, steroids can be very harmful. In a weird way they speed up the body's natural aging processes so that a hereditary condition like high blood pressure, which ordinarily wouldn't be a problem until middle-age, becomes a problem *now*. And they're habit-forming, if not addictive. Two undergraduate guys in my dorm were kicked off the football team for using steroids. If your friend keeps taking them, he could be throwing his whole track career down the drain." Beth sighed. "He's taking a big risk just to shave a second or two off his time."

"I don't believe it," Annie whispered. "Beth, what am I going to do?"

"I don't know." Beth shook her head. "You've got to try to get him to stop. But if he's been taking steroids for a while, he's probably less reasonable and more defensive than he was before the steroids. It won't be easy. But I'll tell you one thing, Annie. If you really care about this guy, you've got to talk to him."

Annie paced the living room for what seemed like the hundredth time that evening. Since her lunch with Beth earlier, she'd been a nervous wreck. It had taken all her courage to call Tony and ask him to come over. He'd been distant on the phone and reluctant to accept her invitation. She'd told him she had something very important she needed to talk to him about. Did he think she was going to break up with him? Annie almost laughed aloud. Maybe she was going to break up with him. A lot would depend on Tony, on his reaction to what she had to tell him.

Mrs. Whitman and her boyfriend had gone out for an early Sunday dinner. Annie continued to pace, hoping they wouldn't come home before she and Tony were finished. *Nice way to put it*, Annie thought as she checked her watch again.

Just then, the doorbell rang and Annie started. She opened the door slowly.

Tony stood in the hallway, a nervous smile fixed on his handsome face. "Hi," he said.

"Hi." Annie stepped back from the door. "Come on in."

Tony nodded and followed Annie into the apartment.

"Thanks for coming over," Annie said quickly. "Do you want something to drink?"

"No, thanks. Listen, Annie, I really don't have a lot of time—"

Annie cut him off with a shake of her head. "I know, Tony. I know that lately all you have time for is running, that all you think about is running."

Tony looked uncomfortable and sat down awkwardly on the edge of an armchair. "Yeah, well, I guess that's true." He looked up and met Annie's eyes; his own were suddenly filled with passion. "But right now, that's the most important thing to me—running and my track career. You don't understand what it's like, Annie. I'd do anything to make it, to prove to my father I can win big. I'd even—"

"Take steroids?"

Annie watched as Tony's face registered the shock he felt at hearing her accusation. Then she watched as the look of surprise became one of defensiveness and denial.

"What do you mean by that?" Tony asked, placing his hands on his knees as if to hold himself down.

"I know, Tony. I know that you've been taking steroids," Annie replied quietly as she sat down in the armchair facing his.

"I don't know what you mean, Annie. I haven't been taking steroids." Tony's voice was controlled and even. Annie knew what a great effort it was costing him to stay calm.

"Listen, Tony. I'm not going to tell anyone else. But I had to tell you that I know—"

Before Annie could continue, Tony was on his feet and halfway to the door. Suddenly he turned and looked back at her. Annie kept her face averted.

"For the last time, Annie, I don't care what you think you know. You're wrong. The only drug I'm taking is something Dr. Griffin prescribed for me. *That's all*. Understand?"

"Tony, I only want to help—"

Once again Tony's voice, now strained, cut her off. "Look, I don't need your help. I don't need anyone's help. And for the last time, I am *not* taking steroids!"

Annie heard him yank open the door and slam it shut behind him. She sat silently, without moving, for what seemed like a very long time. Well, she had tried. She had tried to get him to admit to her that he was in trouble. But he had denied everything she knew to be true. It occurred to her that maybe Tony really didn't know he was taking steroids, though that seemed unlikely.

She knew she should tell Coach Featherston or the Estebans. Tony always spoke so highly of his father. Surely Mr. Esteban would know what to do? But Annie also knew she couldn't turn him in. In spite of everything, she loved Tony. She would just have to figure out some other way to get Tony to stop taking steroids—before it was too late.

Eleven

For several days, Annie kept what she had learned from Beth, and the disastrous results of her meeting with Tony to herself. When she was with Tony, she tried to act as if nothing had changed between them, as if she believed every word he'd said, even as if their confrontation on Sunday night had never happened. *He probably doesn't even remember it*, Annie thought wryly. The All-County meet was two weeks from that coming Saturday, and Tony was completely absorbed in practice.

On Wednesday afternoon a group of kids were having lunch together. After a while Winston left to do some research for a paper, and Tony excused himself to finish his homework so he'd be free to spend the whole afternoon on the track. A few minutes later Todd got up, too. "I might as well join Winston in the library," he said.

Once Todd had gone, Annie, Elizabeth, and Roger were left alone at the table.

"How's Mitch?" Elizabeth asked Roger.

"OK. His month of suspension ends this week. He's going back to L.A. this weekend," Roger said. "Only he's made arrangements to come back for the All-County meet. He's turned into a real track fanatic." Roger frowned. "But he's still pretty bummed out about what happened Saturday night. I wish Tony would apologize to him before he goes home."

"What happened?" Elizabeth asked curiously.

"It's a long story. Let's just say Tony lost his temper with Mitch," Annie said. She felt a sting of tears in her eyes.

"That doesn't sound like Tony. Was something bothering him?" Elizabeth asked.

Roger shook his head. "It wasn't just an isolated incident. Tony's been pretty uptight lately. Annie, you see more of him than we do. What do you think is going on?"

Annie frowned and, almost before she could begin to formulate an excuse for Tony's recent behavior, she heard the words tumbling out of her mouth. "You guys have to promise not to tell anyone. I've been so confused, and I don't know what to do . . ." Annie's tears came in earnest now, and Elizabeth put her arm around her.

"Calm down, Annie. It's OK. You don't have to tell us anything if you don't want to."

Annie shook her head. "But I *do* want to," she protested. "I need your help." And, falteringly, Annie told Elizabeth and Roger about the pills she'd found in Tony's locker.

"Oh, no," Elizabeth whispered. "Did you confront him yet?"

"That's the really awful part. I did, Sunday night. And he denied he's taking steroids! He said he's only taking the pills his doctor prescribed for him. But I know that's not true." Annie sighed. "I don't know why Tony's trying to deny what's going on, or why he refuses help. I only know I've got to think of *some* way to help him without his finding out. I haven't thought about anything else since I found those pills last week."

"I can't believe Tony would intentionally take steroids," Roger said thoughtfully. "Maybe he *doesn't* know what they are or how dangerous they can be. Tony's got far too much riding on this season to throw it away on something as stupid as steroids."

Elizabeth nodded. "There's got to be some way . . ."

"I know!" Roger snapped his fingers. "Listen," he said softly. "I saw this on a late-night movie once. You can have pills made to look exactly like the real things. They're called placebos, pills with nothing in them but sugar. If they're made carefully, Tony shouldn't be able

117

to spot the difference between the placebos and the steroids he's been taking. Once you have them made, all you have to do is sneak back into Tony's locker and swap the pills. Tony will stop taking steroids without even knowing he's stopped. Sometime later you can tell him what you did."

"But how am I supposed to get pills that look identical to the ones he's taking?" Annie asked skeptically. "And won't he notice the difference? Won't he start running slower?"

"No," Elizabeth said excitedly. "If Tony *thinks* he's still taking pills that make him stronger or faster, there may not be any difference in his strength or speed. When he discovers the truth, he'll realize he never needed steroids in the first place."

"It's not a bad idea. I could ask my cousin Beth to help me." Annie looked anxiously from Roger to Elizabeth. "And you won't say a word about this to anyone?"

"Not a single word," Elizabeth promised.

"Me, neither," Roger said. "No wonder Tony's been behaving strangely. I don't know who got him started on steroids, but whoever it is should have his head examined. With a drill."

Roger met Tony after school on Friday. They had half an hour before practice, and Roger knew it was the only opportunity Tony would have to see Mitch before he left the next day for Los Angeles.

Tony rummaged through his locker. "I don't get it," he muttered. "I could swear I left them in here." He yanked out a sweater, glared at it, and stuffed it back inside the locker.

Roger hadn't been with Annie and Elizabeth when they'd substituted the placebos for the steroids, but they told him it had gone as planned. On Thursday, Annie's cousin Beth had made the placebos of sugar and food coloring in her lab. She had been able to match the steroid pills so perfectly that neither Annie nor Elizabeth had been able to tell which was which.

That morning Annie and Elizabeth had gotten to school early and had made the switch. Apparently they hadn't put the bottle back in exactly the same place.

"Phew," Tony said at last as he seized a small plastic bottle and shoved it in his pocket. He turned to Roger and said quickly, "Just some painkillers the doctor gave me. My knee still twinges every once in a while, and I don't want to risk it not being perfect for the big meet."

Roger nodded and fell in place beside Tony as they walked toward the locker room.

"Listen, Tony, Mitch is here. He was hoping to talk to you before he went back home," Roger said abruptly.

"I don't see why he wants to talk to me,"

Tony said. "Anyway, I don't really have anything to say to him."

Roger took a deep breath. "Look, Mitch came to Sweet Valley with a lot of strikes against him. You made a big impression on him. You're all he's talked about since he got here. He idolizes you. And what happened last weekend at the bowling alley really hurt him. Mitch didn't cheat. He was only trying to win, the way you taught him. And you lashed out at him and made him feel like a nothing."

"I didn't mean to," Tony said softly. "I like Mitch. He's a good kid. I guess I should tell him I'm sorry."

"He's been saving money to buy a bike, but he's decided to use it instead to come back in two weeks and watch you run," Roger continued.

"All right. I'll say goodbye to him." Tony glanced self-consciously at Roger. "But I want to talk to him alone."

"OK." Roger smiled at his friend. "He's waiting for you outside, near the bike racks."

Tony took a deep breath. He didn't know what to say to Mitch. The more he thought about it, the more absurd it seemed that he could have yelled at a thirteen-year-old over something as unimportant as a friendly game of bowling. What had gone through his head that night? Had he really suspected Mitch of cheating? Or had the frustration of knowing his team was losing made him lose control?

Tony saw Mitch waiting for him by the bike racks. With his back to Tony and his shoulders a little hunched, Mitch looked so vulnerable that Tony felt ashamed of himself for his earlier behavior.

"Hey, Mitch," he said. Tony came up behind Mitch and put his hand on the boy's shoulder.

Mitch jumped. The expression of happiness on his face when he turned around made Tony feel even worse.

"Hey!" Mitch said. "Thanks for coming out here, man. I know you've got practice and everything. Did Roger tell you I'm coming back to see your big meet?"

"Yeah." Tony sat down next to Mitch. "You looking forward to going home?" he asked after what seemed like a long silence.

Mitch bit his lip. "I dunno." He shrugged. "I kind of like being here. Roger's a good guy. You know," he added awkwardly. "And being around you and everything."

Tony took a deep breath. "Listen, Mitch, I owe you an apology. I was wrong the other night at the bowling alley when I accused you of cheating. I've, well, I've had a lot on my mind lately, and I guess it made me lose my temper." Tony cleared his throat. "I'm really sorry."

"Maybe I did step over the line," Mitch said uncertainly.

Tony felt a lump forming in his throat. "No, Mitch. I'm the one who stepped over the line."

121

"You're just trying to be nice. Listen, I'm *always* in trouble, always doing something wrong," Mitch insisted. "I've got all sorts of problems. The counselor at school is always telling me that."

Tony didn't know what to say to the boy. He didn't know what he was like when he was home in Los Angeles. But he did know that while he had been in Sweet Valley Mitch had kept his word about not drinking and had won the respect of Tony and others.

Unconsciously, Tony reached into his pocket. His hand closed around the bottle of pills. Then he looked at the frank expression on Mitch's face.

"I wish I could be like you, Tony," Mitch said hurriedly. "If I were good at something, like you're good at running, I'd be so happy." Mitch cleared his throat. "And I've been thinking a lot about all that stuff you said to me about not breaking rules and about how the rules are there to protect me. And I want you to know, I think what you said makes a lot of sense. Especially about drinking."

Tony tightened his hand around the bottle of pills. *I managed to convince Mitch to stop drinking,* he thought miserably. *And at the same time I'm buying pills I pretend not to know are steroids!*

Tony felt sick at heart. Mitch was a kid with real problems. He didn't have a devoted father, as Tony did. He didn't have a brilliant sports career ahead of him. But he was willing to stop drinking, to try to clean up his life and make something of himself. The irony of their situations made Tony feel like crying.

"I'm going to miss you, Mitch," Tony said quickly.

"Hey, listen," Mitch said. "Cool it, OK? I told you I'm coming back in two weeks to see you run."

"Yeah," Tony said dully.

All of Mitch's bike money, spent to watch him compete. Tony sighed. He wished he didn't feel like such a sham.

Twelve

Elizabeth was in excellent spirits on Saturday. She spent the morning shopping for some last-minute things, including a new bottle of perfume, for her special date that night with Todd.

"You're sure in a good mood," Jessica muttered when Elizabeth got home around noon. "You're probably just glad you don't have to spend the afternoon talking to the Rotary Club about the joys of being Miss Teen Sweet Valley." She grimaced. "I think I liked life better *before* my career as a beauty queen."

Elizabeth giggled. "Serves you right," was all the consolation she could offer. "Jess, which outfit do you think is more romantic?" she demanded. She tugged her sister into her bedroom and pointed to the clothes she'd laid out on her bed.

Jessica frowned. "Too conservative," she said

after she had inspected the first outfit, a blue cotton jumper and white blouse. "This is much more romantic," she said, pointing to the second option, a printed cotton halter dress. "What's the occasion?" she asked curiously.

"I'll tell you tomorrow." Elizabeth's eyes twinkled. "I'm afraid I'll jinx the whole thing if I say a word." '

But how could anything possibly go wrong? she asked herself later as she luxuriated in a bubble bath. Annie and Enid were ready to trap Todd at his house at six o'clock. The plan was simple. They would tell Todd that Elizabeth's car had broken down and that she needed help, and then they'd drive him out toward Castillo San Angelo. Ten minutes from the castillo, they would turn into a gas station, pounce on Todd, blindfold him, and tell him that he was a hostage to romance!

Elizabeth had to congratulate herself. It was a perfect plan. She'd even gone along with Todd's ho-hum plans to go roller-skating with a big crowd of people that night. He didn't suspect a thing.

Roller-skating with a crowd, she thought. No way! She and Todd would be sitting on the garden patio of Castillo San Angelo. Just the two of them, at last!

At five minutes to six, Enid called to tell Elizabeth that she and Annie were on their way to Todd's house.

"We'll deliver him to you at Castillo San Angelo by seven-fifteen," Enid promised.

Elizabeth fastened her earrings and headed downstairs to leave. When she reached the front hall, the doorbell rang.

Elizabeth glanced down at Prince Albert. "Who can that be?" she asked him. Her parents were out shopping, and Jessica would use her keys.

"Winston!" she exclaimed as she opened the front door.

"Liz, hi. Can I come in for a second?" Winston asked.

"Sure," Elizabeth said, noticing the look of concern on Winston's face.

"I don't want to scare you, and everything's going to be just fine. But you've got to come with me. Todd's had an accident," Winston said.

"Wh—what?" Elizabeth stammered.

"He's going to be OK. He's just worried because he said he had plans to meet you in an hour—"

All thoughts of Castillo San Angelo vanished. "Winston, where is he? What happened?" Elizabeth cried.

"Come on. I've got my car out front," Winston said. Without another word, Elizabeth grabbed her keys and raced out the front door with him.

"Tell me exactly what happened," Elizabeth

126

commanded as Winston pulled his car out onto the highway a few minutes later.

"I don't really know. All Todd told me was that he borrowed a motorcycle from a friend of his and rode a little farther than he had planned. He sounded like he was just badly shaken up. And the bike is ruined."

Elizabeth frowned. "That's not like Todd. He promised his parents he wouldn't ride a motorcycle after that bad accident we had earlier this year."

Winston shrugged. "I guess he just, you know, sort of slipped a little."

Elizabeth glanced at the road signs they were passing. San Grandida. San Manuel. *That's weird*, she thought. They were traveling along the route she would have taken to get to Castillo San Angelo.

"We'd better stop for gas," Winston said after checking the gauge. Before Elizabeth could respond, Winston had turned off into a gas station.

"Do me a favor. Go in and buy me a chocolate bar," Winston said, gesturing toward the snack shop.

Suddenly Elizabeth felt terribly confused. This just wasn't making sense. How did Winston know where Todd was? If he was so worried, why stop to think about a chocolate bar? And she just couldn't believe Todd would borrow someone's motorcycle. Not after the promise he'd made to his parents.

127

All of these thoughts were racing through her mind as she left the snack shop with Winston's chocolate bar. But she didn't get very far.

"Surprise!" Winston said gruffly. He stepped up behind her and quickly tied something soft around her eyes.

"Winston, what on earth do you think you're doing?" Elizabeth cried.

"You're being kidnapped, that's what," Winston said proudly. "Under strict orders of a Mr. Todd Wilkins. Now turn around and let me tie up your hands. And if I were you, I wouldn't bother to struggle."

For the next fifteen minutes Elizabeth tried to convince Winston that everything was now a complete mess. "*Todd's* the one who's being kidnapped! Winston, you guys have ruined everything!" she cried. What was going to happen when Enid and Annie got Todd to Castillo San Angelo and she wasn't there? "I want you to take this ridiculous blindfold off me," she insisted. "I'm not kidding, Winston. Stop the car, untie me, and get this dumb thing off my eyes."

"You're not supposed to make a peep. I've seen this in movies," Winston instructed. "Just lie back in the seat and moan every once in a while."

"Winston, I'm serious," Elizabeth cried again.

"You're a rotten person to kidnap, Liz," Winston said jovially about ten minutes later. Elizabeth thought they might have turned off the highway, but she couldn't be sure.

"Mmm," Winston said. "Smell that? It's honeysuckle."

There are honeysuckle trees at Castillo San Angelo, Elizabeth remembered. But all that was ruined now. Todd was there without her. And she was stuck here, wherever she was, without him.

"Madam, your kidnapper awaits you," Winston said with mock gravity. He turned off the engine and came around to the back seat to release her.

Elizabeth couldn't believe her eyes as she got out of the car. "But . . ." For once in her life she was speechless.

They were at Castillo San Angelo! It looked just like it looked in the pictures, only more beautiful. Tiny white lights were strung on the mimosa and honeysuckle trees in the luxurious gardens. The terrace was set up with lovely tables, and behind the splendor of the European-style castle were the San Angelo mountains. It was breathtaking.

"That's strange. Todd was supposed to be here already," Winston said, scratching his head.

"I told you. He's been kidnapped," Elizabeth said with a giggle.

"You mean you weren't kidding about Todd's being kidnapped, too?"

"Don't worry," Elizabeth said. "I have a feeling he'll be here any minute."

Maybe the surprise she'd planned for Todd wouldn't be as much of a surprise as she'd hoped. But it was worth it, Elizabeth thought, when a few minutes later she saw the stunned expression on Todd's face when Annie and Enid deposited him in the parking lot.

"I don't get it," Enid said to Winston. "What are *you* doing here? *We're* the kidnappers."

"I could ask you the same thing," Winston said. "And *I'm* the kidnapper."

"But how—?" Annie looked at Todd. "How did *you* know about this place?"

"Winston," Todd moaned, "when you told me you'd found the perfect place for a romantic getaway, you didn't tell me you'd found it through Liz!"

"My guidebook!" Annie cried.

"Maybe you two really are suited for each other after all," Enid said laughingly to Elizabeth and Todd. "How many people could come up with the same scheme the way you two did?"

"But I wanted to surprise you!" Elizabeth wailed.

"And *I* wanted to surprise *you*," Todd echoed. "I wanted to pounce!"

"I guess we both wanted to pounce," Elizabeth admitted.

Annie laughed. "It's really funny. You both

come up with the same idea for the same place on the same night."

"But our blindfold was better," Winston said, holding up a pair of magenta pantyhose. "More colorful, anyway. I think Todd and I get first prize."

"No way, Winston. Annie and I were wonderful. We *terrified* Todd," Enid retorted. "Didn't we?" She looked to Annie for confirmation. "And we even tried to gag him, but he told us the rag we used tasted really gross."

"Look, as long as we're all here safe and sound," Winston said, "why don't we go in and have dinner together?"

Elizabeth and Todd looked at each other and in perfect unison cried, *"No!"*

"I don't think that was an invitation, Winston," Enid said dryly. "But I'll tell you what. Leave your car for Todd and Liz. You come back with Annie and me, and we'll treat you to a burger on the way."

"Yeah." Annie snatched the magenta pantyhose from Winston's hands. "Agree, or we'll blindfold you and take you back against your will."

"OK, OK," Winston said, letting Annie and Enid lead him away. "I know when I'm not wanted."

"Listen," Todd said softly when the others had gone, "we've both gone to a lot of trouble to have a wonderful evening together. Now let's enjoy ourselves. Should we go up to the terrace and have dinner?"

"What a wonderful idea," Elizabeth said, taking his hand.

The maitre d' gave them a haughty look when they reached the terrace restaurant. "I certainly hope you made reservations," he said.

"We did," Elizabeth answered. "As a matter of fact, we made them twice!"

It was a magical evening. The food was delicious, and the atmosphere romantic. Todd raised his glass for a toast.

"To being alone together," he murmured.

"To romance," Elizabeth concurred.

"To great minds thinking alike," he said with a smile.

"To you and me, Todd Wilkins," Elizabeth whispered. It gave her a warm feeling, knowing they'd had the same fantasy. And an even warmer feeling knowing that together they had made it come true!

Mitch Ferguson went back to Los Angeles on Saturday morning, but Tony just couldn't stop thinking about him. He hung around the house most of the day, listening to some old records and trying not to think about the kid. No one had ever idolized him. How ironic that it should happen at a time when he felt so unworthy of being idolized.

That night he helped his father make a barbecue. It was one of the few times they'd been alone together in weeks.

"You're looking good, son. I bet you're excited about the All-County meet," Mr. Esteban said.

Tony wished he could tell his father the truth. Maybe his father would know what to do about the mess he'd gotten himself into. The burden of carrying the secret around with him was getting harder and harder to bear.

"A couple of the guys at work want to come watch you run," he continued proudly. "I told them all that Burr Davidson would be there. Next stop, the Olympics!" Mr. Esteban clapped his hand on Tony's shoulder. "I'm so proud of you, Tony. Sometimes I almost feel as if it's *me* out there on the track!"

Tony bit his lip. So much for telling his father the truth. All his life his father had dreamed of this moment of glory. If Tony blew the big race, he wouldn't just be throwing away his own career. He'd be throwing away his father's all over again.

When Tony finished dinner he excused himself and went upstairs to his bedroom. He slipped a green pill out of the bottle and squinted at it, as if close scrutiny could tell him something about its contents. Maybe it really *was* just a special vitamin. In middle school Tony had had a coach who claimed you could take anything, and as long as you believed it would make you stronger and faster, it would. Just because Lou had been acting secretive about his selling the pills didn't necessarily mean they were illegal, did it? Wasn't it possible Lou just hyped the whole thing in order to make lots of money selling the pills?

Tony headed down the hall to the bathroom and poured himself a glass of water. He could almost hear Mitch's voice explaining how he had realized that drinking was wrong—thanks to Tony.

Tony threw his head back and popped the pill in his mouth. *Some role model.*

On Thursday afternoon, a week and two days before the All-County meet, Tony went to the gym to work with leg weights. He was relieved that Lou wasn't there.

He worked out for about forty minutes, took a quick shower, and headed out to the locker room to change. Suddenly he heard angry voices from a few aisles away. Tony froze when he recognized Lou's voice.

"Look, Randy, you knew the risks when you started taking the stuff. I'm sorry you got caught, but I told you not to take them in front of anyone. A coach! I'm surprised you made it this long without being caught!"

Tony felt his heart sink as he listened.

Randy's voice was shaking. "It's my whole life, Lou. It's not just one season. Steroids are illegal! You didn't tell me that when you started selling them to me. Remember what you told me? That they're exactly the same stuff doctors prescribe? Well, they're not. You're full of it, Lou. And you had better watch it, that's all I can say. I just might take you down with me."

Tony jumped when a locker door was slammed shut. He didn't wait to hear more. Grabbing his things, he ran back into the shower room.

He couldn't deny it anymore. He'd been taking steroids. *Steroids.* Tony, who had never touched a beer his whole life, who didn't even like to take an aspirin unless he absolutely had to!

His first sensation was one of pure shame. How could he face anyone again? His parents, his friends, Mitch, Annie? Especially Annie. Somehow, she had known all along. She had been smarter than he had been, by far. Would she ever forgive him for the way he had rejected her offer of help?

Tony took a deep breath. *Look*, he said to himself. *You've got to do something. You've got to get your life back.*

Tony knew there were a few things he'd have to do right away. He'd have to tell Coach Featherston he couldn't run in the All-County meet. He couldn't let himself participate, not if steroids were what had enabled him to qualify for the meet in the first place.

But first, he had to tell his father the truth.

Thirteen

"I just don't understand." Mr. Esteban jammed his hands in his pockets and began to pace. "You're telling me you took these pills for weeks without even knowing what they were?"

"I didn't want to know." Tony hung his head. "I knew they were making me faster, and that's all I cared about." A lump formed in Tony's throat. "Dad, I wanted to win for you as much as for me! For the past few months all you've talked about is the Olympics, Burr Davidson, talent scouts. When I got hurt, I felt as if I had ruined *your* career as much as mine."

Mr. Esteban was silent for a long time. When he turned to look at Tony, there were tears in his eyes. "You're right, son," he said quietly. "I've been trying to relive my old sports career through you. Because I had to drop out, I've pushed you to do what I never could." He shrugged. "Who knows? Maybe getting onto the Olympic team isn't something you ever really wanted."

Tony stared down at the carpet. It was hard to talk so honestly to his father, but at the same time it was a real relief. All the things he'd been keeping bottled up for so long were out in the open at last.

"I *do* want the Olympics, Dad. At least I want to try. I want to be the best runner I can be. But these past couple of weeks, I've realized the hard way that winning isn't the only thing. Shaving a couple of seconds off your time isn't worth losing your self-respect."

Mr. Esteban crossed the room to sit on the sofa next to his son. "You know, Tony, sometimes parents aren't as smart as their children. You've taught me something tonight. Your turning to steroids was as much my mistake as yours. If I hadn't been pushing you so hard, I might have been able to see that you needed me. That you were in trouble."

"I threw them out," Tony said. He shook his head ruefully. "The funny thing is, they probably didn't even do that much for me physically. I read some literature on steroids this afternoon. Supposedly it takes longer than only a few weeks to produce any physical changes. Most of what I've been experiencing has been psychological. I *thought* they'd make me stronger and faster, so I *became* stronger and faster."

137

"Let's just be thankful that you decided to stop taking them before they hurt you."

"I think they *have* hurt me," Tony said slowly. "I'm going to have to withdraw from the All-County meet."

"You feel it's not fair to compete because you've been using steroids?"

Tony nodded. "I know I'm letting you down, Dad. And I'm sorry," he whispered.

Mr. Esteban put his arm around Tony and hugged him. "Listen to me," he said gruffly. "I've never been so proud of you, OK? So cut out the let-me-down nonsense. In my book you're a champion."

Tony felt the tears sting his eyes. He knew that withdrawing from the meet was the right thing to do. But he couldn't believe how much it hurt.

"So that's the story," Tony said to Annie Friday night at Guido's. "I'm going to talk to Coach Featherston tomorrow."

Annie stared down at the table. She couldn't believe what Tony had just told her. He'd finally confessed to everything. Buying the magic vitamins from Lou, suspecting they might be steroids, but continuing to take them anyway.

"You know, I never thought I'd end up in a situation like this. But I've learned something," Tony said slowly. "I never thought I could be desperate enough to take drugs or to drink. I never once thought about taking steroids—until I got hurt, that is. And then I lost my confidence. I was afraid it would take forever for my knee to heal. I felt I had so much riding on this season that I just couldn't risk falling behind." He shook his head. "I'll tell you one thing, Annie. I owe a big thanks to Mitch Ferguson. That kid really woke me up. Hearing my own words from his mouth really helped to open my eyes."

Annie took Tony's hand in hers. "I've missed you, Tony," she said simply. "You've seemed like a stranger these past few weeks. I'm glad to have you back."

Tony took a deep breath.

"It's a relief to be able to talk about this, Annie. Particularly after what happened that Sunday night at your apartment. I still don't know how you knew I was taking steroids. I mean, at that point, I *think* I knew, but I was still fooling myself, still hoping I was wrong. I can't believe you were so *sure*."

Annie glanced down at the table again. "Tony, listen. I've got to tell you something important. You're not the only one who has something to confess." She lifted her head and looked uneasily at him. How could she tell him what she'd done without making him furious with her? "I guess the best way is just to tell you straight out. I didn't just figure out or assume from your behavior you were taking steroids. I *knew*."

"But how?" Tony seemed stunned.

"I'm not very proud of the way I found out," Annie said quickly. "Remember when you gave me the combination to your locker?"

Tony nodded, and Annie went on. "One day when I was looking for a book to loan to Elizabeth, I found a bottle of pills." Annie took a deep breath. "I was confused. I was pretty sure you'd finished the doctor's prescription. And I was worried. So I took one of the pills from the bottle. A cousin of mine is a biochemist, and I knew she'd run some tests on the pills if I asked her for help." Annie looked anxiously at Tony and hurried on. "Once I knew that the pills were steroids and she described some of the negative effects they might have, I just knew I had to talk with you before going any further on my own. But you didn't want to listen. You denied everything, even the possibility that you were taking steroids without knowing it. When you stormed out of my apartment, I was frightened. I thought it was all over between us. And then, the next day, we *both* acted as if nothing had happened! That's when I got really frightened, and I knew I had to do something."

"So you knew," Tony said quietly.

Annie laughed nervously and continued. "And I'm not the only one who knew after that."

"Who else?" Tony looked miserable.

"Elizabeth and Roger."

For a minute Tony was quiet. "Did *you* tell them?"

"I needed their help," she whispered.

"I wish you hadn't," Tony said.

"There's more," Annie continued miserably. "We got my cousin to make placebos. They're harmless, made out of sugar and food coloring. And we swapped them with the ones in your locker. So for the past week you haven't been taking steroids, Tony. I know you're probably never going to want to talk to me again," she said hurriedly, her eyes filling with tears. "But before you talk to Coach Featherston and throw away your chance of winning the All-County meet, I wanted you to know."

"I don't know what to say," Tony said quietly.

"None of us knew what to do. We were all so scared," Annie rushed on. "I wanted to help you, Tony. I care so much about you."

Tony shook his head. "This is a lot to handle all at once. You mean, for the past seven days I've been taking sugar pills?"

"We switched them last Friday. So yeah, since then your scores have been good because *you've* been good," Annie said. She fiddled with her bracelet, afraid to look at him. "I guess you're pretty mad at me. But I want you to think about what I've said before you talk to the coach. Maybe it can still work out for you."

Tony nodded. "Maybe," he said.

For a long moment neither of them spoke. "Listen, Annie. I'm not sure how I feel or what I want to do." Tony pushed back his chair. "I know we're supposed to spend the evening together, but I think I should just take you home."

"I understand," Annie said woodenly.

It was what she had expected. But even so, it was hard to say good night to him when he dropped her off half an hour later. She had tried to save Tony's career. Maybe she had succeeded. But she knew he wasn't going to thank her for it.

"Tony, you've made a serious mistake," Coach Featherston said on Sunday afternoon. He was sitting behind the desk in his study at home, hands folded behind his neck. "We're six days away from the meet that could decide your future. This is hard to hear right now."

"I know, sir. I'm only telling you because I don't think it's fair for me to enter the meet Saturday unless I get the all-clear."

Coach Featherston swiveled slowly in his chair. "I'll talk to Coach Schultz. We'll have to assemble the county coaches . . . check the athletic department rules. . . . You'll have to undergo blood tests to determine what level of steroids are in your system."

"I know all that." Tony shifted his weight from one foot to the other. "I've made a chart indicating the day I started taking the pills, the day my girlfriend substituted the fake ones, the whole thing."

Coach Featherston took the sheet of paper Tony held out to him and looked it over with a sigh. "Well, all I can do is call an emergency meeting and go from there."

"Thanks, Coach," Tony said.

"Tony," Coach Featherston said as Tony turned and started to walk away. "How did you get mixed up in something like this?"

Tony shook his head. "The scary thing is, I'm not really sure. I was frightened and impatient after I got hurt. But I don't know how I was stupid enough to take pills without knowing what they were." He sighed. "You know how you used to tell us that the real winners are the ones who'll do anything to win? I think I took that advice too far. I wanted to qualify for the Olympics more than anything in the world. My father . . ." His voice broke off, but he plodded on. "My dad had a chance to play pro football when he was young. He gave it all up to take care of my grandmother when she was dying. I wanted to win for him *and* for me."

Coach Featherston nodded. "I understand," he said quietly. "The young man at the gym who sold you these steroids—we're going to need his name, son. What he's doing is against the law."

Tony nodded. "I'm willing to tell you, sir. I don't want anyone else getting hurt the way I did."

Coach Featherston stood up and put out his hand. "Tony, I respect you for coming here and telling me the truth. You could have run on Saturday, and no one would have known."

"*I* would have known," Tony said.

Tony felt surprisingly good as he left the coach's house. But he didn't feel like going straight home. He felt like dropping by Annie's apartment just to see if she was around.

It had been a long, long time since he'd treated Annie the way she deserved to be treated. She was a good friend and a loving girlfriend. It felt like a pretty good time for a new beginning.

Elizabeth and Todd arrived for the All-County meet on Saturday morning. "See what great benefits there are to a stroll on the beach at dawn?" Elizabeth asked Todd as she snuggled up against him on the bleachers. "We had time to be alone together and to get here before the mob!"

Todd hugged her close. "I like our new, romantic selves," he whispered. "But reality is about to intrude. Annie Whitman is on her way to interrupt us."

Elizabeth sat up straight and waved to Annie. "She must be excited! Do you think Tony can still pull it off?"

Todd didn't have time to reply before Annie was sitting next to them.

144

"How's Tony feeling? Is he ready?" Elizabeth asked.

"I think so! I'm so glad the coaches decided to let him run," Annie said warmly. "When we got the news last night, I thought Tony was going to jump through the ceiling with excitement."

"So they're not going to penalize him at all?" Todd asked.

"He's on probation for the rest of the season. He had to take two different blood tests, and the results showed he hadn't taken steroids long enough to have changed his performance substantially. He really only took them for less than three weeks, and his doctor believes most of the positive effects he felt were psychological."

Elizabeth nodded. "And what about the guy who sold the steroids to Tony?"

"The police are still investigating his case," Annie said. "At the very least, he'll be subject to a fine, and he won't be participating in wrestling matches anymore. He *may* have to spend time in jail." She shook her head. "When I think of the number of people one guy like that can hurt, I get so angry!"

"Well, let's just be glad the coaches let Tony run today." Elizabeth's eyes brightened. "I just know he's going to win!"

"Hey, look. Burr Davidson is here," Todd exclaimed. "And here comes one of Tony's most loyal fans," Todd added. He waved to

Mitch, who was climbing up the bleachers to join them.

"Listen, I'm going down to give Tony a kiss before the meet gets started. See you guys later," Annie said as she hurried away.

"We didn't tell her that we may sneak off, just the two of us," Elizabeth whispered to Todd.

"Yeah. Back to Castillo San Angelo, for instance," Todd whispered back, holding her hand tightly in his.

A minute later both of them erupted in laughter when Mitch clambered up and sat down in between them. They could laugh at the intrusion now and not worry about having their solitude infringed upon. Both Elizabeth and Todd had learned that as long as they cared enough about making room for each other, there was nothing wrong with being a twosome in a crowd!

"Are you OK?" Roger asked Tony.

Tony nodded. "I'm worried about Rex Olson, though." Rex was the strongest runner in the state, and his event was the 220. He wasn't going to be easy to beat.

One glance around the crowded bleachers proved to Tony that this meet was as important as he'd been telling himself it would be. The place was virtually crawling with talent scouts, including Burr Davidson, as well as coaches, fans, friends, and family. Tony could see his father and mother up in the bleachers, both of them looking as proud as if Tony had already won. He knew now that to them he was a champion no matter what.

"Look, Mitch made it," Roger said. He waved up at the bleachers.

Tony's heart swelled as he, too, waved at Mitch, who held up a handmade placard that said, in simple bold letters, TONY.

The 220 was scheduled for eleven o'clock. Time seemed to crawl between nine and ten-thirty, and then suddenly the minutes raced by and it was eleven. Rex came forward, wearing the green-and-gold uniform of Western High.

Tony crouched down at the starting line. For one crazy moment a zillion things rushed through his mind. Would he trip again? Would he run as fast as before? Then, a second before the firing of the starting gun, a pleasant numbness came over him. And then he heard a clear, high voice calling his name, and he knew it was Mitch.

The gun fired and he was off. He felt as if he was running for all of them—for Annie, for his parents, and for Mitch. Mitch, who had reminded him that what mattered most was not if you won, but *how* you won.

Tony felt his breath tearing in his lungs as he approached the first bend. Rex was pulling ahead of him. There was nothing else but arms and legs and panting, and then suddenly he was pulling forward. He felt something in him break free, and it was as if he was running through his own limitations. And then he was over the finish line.

He'd won. And when he heard his time, he realized he'd beaten the state record.

His arms lifted in the air in a victory salute, and the Sweet Valley High crowd went crazy. Tony searched for Annie's face and raised his fist. She raised hers back. He knew this was a moment he'd never forget. This wasn't just a race he'd won. It was much, much more. Hearing the cheers of the people around him, Tony felt as if his heart would burst with joy. He knew now that magic didn't come from pills. Magic was something you made yourself.

On Monday at lunchtime, the crowd gathered in the cafeteria was still talking about Tony's win at the All-County meet on Saturday.

"I have to thank you personally, Tony," Elizabeth said. She pulled a piece of paper from her folder and waved it in the air. "Your fabulous victory provided me with a great story for *The Oracle.* Who knows? You may have a shot at the Olympics, and after this article hits the papers, I may have a career in sports journalism!"

"Well, you and Tony won't be the only ones out on the field," Winston said. He crossed his arms and looked slyly around the table. "For the price of an ice-cream sandwich, I'll tell you all I know about a certain football player whose career seemed to be sidelined for good."

Todd mimicked Winston's crossed arms and crafty look. "Do you mean you'll tell us that Scott Trost has been reinstated as second-string quarterback on the Gladiators?"

Winston groaned. "Thanks a lot, Wilkins! Now I'll have to starve."

Annie sighed and looked at Enid. "What do you say, Enid? We bail him out again?"

"Sure. It's only the second time this month we'll be feeding him."

"Enough about Winston and his stomach!" Roger protested with a laugh. "I want to know more about Scott."

"All I know," Todd said, "is that he managed to pull up his grades, and his suspension from the team was lifted."

"Well, as a guy who was forced to be away from his sport, I can imagine how happy he must be!" Tony said earnestly. "I know our situations were very different, but being kept away from the thing you love more than anything—" Tony put his arm around Annie and grinned sheepishly. "Well, the thing you love *almost* more than anything, is really depressing."

"I'm sure you're right. But I can't really feel anything for Scott," Elizabeth said. "His attitude toward girls is so cavemanlike, it makes me want to scream—or at least give him a good punch in the nose!"

"Me, too!" Annie and Enid chorused.

"I wouldn't be too hard on the guy," Todd said. "He's not as macho as he seems. A lot of it is an act."

"Todd's right." Winston stood up. "He really doesn't mean any harm."

"I find that a little hard to believe," Enid said dryly. "And if you say one more word in his defense, Winston, you're not getting your ice-cream sandwich."

"OK, OK. Not another word. Money, please." Winston held out his hand and Enid gave him a dollar.

Just then Scott strolled into the cafeteria and caught everyone's attention by letting out a loud wolf whistle. The shy sophomore who was the object of his unwanted attention hurried out of his path, her cheeks flaming with embarrassment.

"Scott's *act* is pretty convincing," Elizabeth said, nodding in Scott's direction.

"Definitely Academy Award material," Enid agreed.

Is Scott Trost as sexist as he seems? Find out in Sweet Valley High #78, THE DATING GAME.

*Celebrate the Seasons
with SWEET VALLEY HIGH
Super Editions*

You've been a SWEET VALLEY HIGH fan all along—hanging out with Jessica and Elizabeth and their friends at Sweet Valley High. And now the SWEET VALLEY HIGH *Super Editions* give you more of what you like best—more romance—more excitement—more real-life adventure! Whether you're bicycling up the California Coast in PERFECT SUMMER, dancing at the Sweet Valley Christmas Ball in SPECIAL CHRISTMAS, touring the South of France in SPRING BREAK, catching the rays in a MALIBU SUMMER, or skiing the snowy slopes in WINTER CARNIVAL—you know you're exactly where you want to be—with the gang from SWEET VALLEY HIGH.

SWEET VALLEY HIGH SUPER EDITIONS

☐ **PERFECT SUMMER**
25072-8/$3.50

☐ **SPRING BREAK**
25537-1/$3.50

☐ **SPECIAL CHRISTMAS**
25377-8/$2.95

☐ **MALIBU SUMMER**
26050-2/$2.95

☐ **WINTER CARNIVAL**
26159-2/$2.95

☐ **SPRING FEVER**
26420-6/$2.95

Series

Don't miss any of the Caitlin trilogies
Created by Francine Pascal

There has never been a heroine quite like the raven-haired, unforgettable beauty, Caitlin. Dazzling, charming, rich, and very, very clever Caitlin Ryan seems to have everything. Everything, that is, but the promise of lasting love. The three trilogies follow Caitlin from her family life at Ryan Acres, to Highgate Academy, the exclusive boarding school in the posh horse country of Virginia, through college, and on to a glamorous career in journalism in New York City.

Don't miss Caitlin!

<u>**THE LOVE TRILOGY**</u>

☐	24716-6	**LOVING #1**	$3.50
☐	25130-9	**LOVE LOST #2**	$3.50
☐	25295-X	**TRUE LOVE #3**	$3.50

Buy them at your local bookstore or use this page to order.

Bantam Books, Dept. CA8, 414 East Golf Road, Des Plaines, IL 60016

Please send me the items I have checked above. I am enclosing $_____ (please add $2.50 to cover postage and handling). Send check or money order, no cash or C.O.D.s please.

Mr/Ms _____

Address _____

City/State _____ Zip _____

CA8–2/91

Please allow four to six weeks for delivery.
Prices and availability subject to change without notice.

☐ 27650	AGAINST THE ODDS #51	$2.95
☐ 27720	WHITE LIES #52	$2.95
☐ 27771	SECOND CHANCE #53	$2.95
☐ 27856	TWO BOY WEEKEND #54	$2.95
☐ 27915	PERFECT SHOT #55	$2.95
☐ 27970	LOST AT SEA #56	$2.95
☐ 28079	TEACHER CRUSH #57	$2.95
☐ 28156	BROKEN HEARTS #58	$2.95
☐ 28193	IN LOVE AGAIN #59	$2.95
☐ 28264	THAT FATAL NIGHT #60	$2.95
☐ 28317	BOY TROUBLE #61	$2.95
☐ 28352	WHO'S WHO #62	$2.95
☐ 28385	THE NEW ELIZABETH #63	$2.95
☐ 28487	THE GHOST OF TRICIA MARTIN #64	$2.95
☐ 28518	TROUBLE AT HOME #65	$2.95
☐ 28555	WHO'S TO BLAME #66	$2.95
☐ 28611	THE PARENT PLOT #67	$2.95
☐ 28618	THE LOVE BET #68	$2.95
☐ 28636	FRIEND AGAINST FRIEND #69	$2.95
☐ 28767	MS. QUARTERBACK #70	$2.95
☐ 28796	STARRING JESSICA #71	$2.95
☐ 28841	ROCK STAR'S GIRL #72	$2.95
☐ 28863	REGINA'S LEGACY #73	$2.95